RESTING WITCH FACE

MAYA DANIELS

By Maya Daniels

Chronicles of Forbidden Witchery

Resting Witch Face
Pitch a Witch
Witch Please
Payback is a Witch

Vinci Books

vinci-books.com

Published by Vinci Books Ltd in 2025

1

Copyright © Maya Daniels 2021

The author has asserted their moral right to be identified as the author of this work in accordance with the Copyright, Designs and Patents Act 1988. This work is a work of fiction. Names, characters, places and incidents are the product of the author's imagination or are used fictitiously. Any resemblance to actual persons, living or dead, places and incidents is entirely coincidental.

All rights reserved. No part of this publication may be copied, reproduced, distributed, stored in any retrieval system, or transmitted in any form or by any means, including photocopying, recording, or other electronic or mechanical methods, nor used as a source for any form of machine learning including AI datasets, without the prior written permission of the publisher.

The publisher and the author have made every effort to obtain permissions for any third party material used in this book and to comply with copyright law. Any queries in this respect should be brought to the attention of the publisher and any omissions will be corrected in future editions.

A CIP catalogue record for this book is available from the British Library.

Paperback ISBN: 9781036705763

Chapter One

Lesson 1: *Don't drink and drive.*

No, scratch that. That was for humans. The real lesson was: don't drink and pretend you're something you are not. Like, acting like a badass witch when you have zero magic. Take it from me because it'll destroy your life. Although that was neither here nor there, when it came to me, since I was screwed the day I popped out of my mother's vagina. She died during childbirth, most probably out of disappointment. I kid you not.

I was a dud born in the most powerful bloodline of witches in the world.

How was that for a sap story?

"Hey, buddy," I called out like we're the best of friends. "Get back down here before you hurt yourself and I get blamed for it. What do you say?" The Kishi demon cocked his head and eyed me like I'd lost my mind. Poor schmuck had no idea that ship had sailed years ago.

My foot wobbled in my designer ankle boots when I

took a step forward, and I did an awkward shimmy-wiggle-swan-dive before I regained my balance. It was what happened when you drank one too many Manhattans and answered a call from your coven to deal with a demon selling illegal merchandise.

"Damn you! If I scratch my boots I'm going to skin you alive just to make myself a new pair. I should've just stayed in the damn bar." The racket of a paint can crashing to the floor and rattling around applauded my muttering. It also stabbed my brain, which was pounding like a shifter in heat when a willing body accidentally stumbled in front of his dick. Don't ask me how I know this, because as brutally honest as I am, I'm not going to tell you.

iPhone held in front of me the same way those pompous asses from the Magi Police waved their badges around, I pointed the flashlight right into the creep's eyes. It screeched like a banshee and scattered further into the darkness while I hissed curses at it. Luckily for the demon, none of them would be taking root, because ... no magic, duh.

What took my coven mates so long to get to the warehouse? If this was a party they'd be lining up at the door since yesterday. As I looked around the dirty warehouse and the misty odor of congealed blood and decaying bodies made my stomach roll, I couldn't say I blamed them.

The fact that Kishi demons had an attractive human face on the front and a hyena's face on the back of their skull was the least of my problems. Kishi demons used their human face as well as their smooth, luring voice and other tricks to attract unassuming idiots— which I definitely was not, shut it I'm not!—and then they proceeded to eat them with their deformed jaws. That would've been fine and dandy if they kept it under wraps, but this one also made an entire collection of body parts to sell on the magical black market. Quite a smart trick when the market was scarce, but not such a great idea for this guy, because he was dumb enough to get caught. That was *if* I managed to hold him back until the others got to the warehouse. With all the alcohol in my blood system, I got this like a hot potato in a bare hand.

Witches more than other supernaturals paid good money for body parts like the ones stacked all the way to the ceiling in the large building, although nobody liked to talk about it. It was that pink elephant in the room we all ignored. No delusions clouded my mind that my coven would "confiscate" the evidence in the warehouse without blinking an eye. I was basically standing in the middle of a gold mine.

The pentagram tattoo on the side of my forefinger tingled, an annoying reminder when my body thought I should be using magic, as adrenaline raced through my veins. My meat suit never got the memo we were shooting blanks. We were as impotent as Mike, my coven's administrator, according to Sissily.

"Go away witch, or die," the demon cooed, his alluring voice gliding over my skin like a caress and leaving goosebumps in its wake.

"Aww, you actually think I'm a witch." My eyelashes fluttered in his general direction as I stumbled deeper into the warehouse. "How adorable," I deadpanned, a serious expression on my face that froze him in his tracks.

Silence followed.

"Ah, you are the useless one." His face poked through the shadows before he fully emerged to sneer at me from over ten feet up, crouched like a gargoyle on the rafters. "I've heard of you. Pathetic." He dismissed me, as his full lip curled over a row of flat, white teeth.

I hated sneering. It reminded me too much of the looks on my coven mates every time they stared in my direction.

Shaking my head to regain my focus, I swallowed hard when the alcohol tried to come up. All I had to do was keep the hellspawn from escaping until reinforcements arrived, but he was pushing his luck. Even a dud could do that if said dud was not a little drunk and teetering on six-inch heels. I eyed my precious boots for a split second, considering using them as a weapon and chucking them at his head, but I changed my mind. Like hell I would mess up a good pair of designer boots for a stupid demon.

The choice was taken from me when he decided to try a trick called monkey in a circus and sailed through the air, aiming his body straight at me. My phone jerked to follow the arch of the jump, and I had one second of an "oh shit" moment before our bodies collided. Never mind me, my iPhone flew from my fingers, crashed on the concrete floor with a resounding crack, and I heard my silk shirt rip at the shoulder when we tumbled on the dirty concrete floor. I just bought that phone.

I saw red.

Fingers hooked like claws, I went straight for his eyes when he tried to straddle me. Somewhere in the back of my mind I was aware that if he bit me the poison from his kind would kill me in less than an hour, but I had liquid courage, louder than the alarm bells cheering me on. The demon didn't expect me to claw at his eyes, so when my nails made squelching mush out of his eyeballs, his human face roared at me. If I was in the right mind, I would be shaking in my skin. As things were, he resembled a chihuahua nipping at my ankles to my muddled brain. Wretchedly vile breath melted my makeup and I gagged, barely holding back the bile so I didn't puke all over both of us.

"It's called a toothbrush, asshole." I hacked hard enough to cough out a lung while jamming my forearm in his throat to hold back his snapping jaws. The Kishi demon was trying to munch on my face, for fuck's sake. "You should use it, damn you."

Desperate times called for desperate measures, and, as much as it pained me, I had to sacrifice my boots. My leg swung up like a slingshot, caught him on the side of the head, and he went down hard. His head bounced off the concrete, and his skull cracked with enough strength to be heard over the heartbeat in my ears. The air whooshing out of him satisfied my need to hurt him like he hurt my poor blouse. It was also new and cost me an arm and a leg. Using the time I had, I scrambled on my knees, yanked my poor boot off, and nailed him in the neck with the heel. The demon gasped, probably still dazed from the kick, but apart from a few spastic jerks, he didn't attempt to flee. Or move again at all, but that would be semantics.

They might think that was how I found him.

Right.

With a sigh, I dropped on my haunches not a moment too soon before the solid thump of feet came from the entrance behind me. Light jiggled up and down over the stacked shelving from the flashlight the person held, and I looked down my shoulder at the flipping piece of silk that used to be a soft olive color. Dirt, sweat, and dried blood from the scrapes on my upper arm turned the silk some disgusting color of brown. I frowned at the flapping fabric.

"Hands up where I can see them," the owner of the flashlight barked from behind me.

Great. Instead of my coven mates, I had to deal with a human cop. Just my luck for the night, it seemed.

"Do I look dangerous to you?" My head twisted so I

could squint at him over my shoulder, and a bright light stabbed me in the brain like a pickaxe. "Are you trying to blind me on purpose, or is this how you pick up chicks all the time? If they have a flashlight burning their retinas they can't see your ugly face, huh?" Oh yeah, I recognized the voice better than I should've.

"Hazel? What in God's name are you doing here?"

"Getting a tan. You?" I chirped brightly and regretted it when acid filled my mouth. I would never drink again.

"Don't be a smartass. I'm seriously asking what—" His words stopped when he noticed my ripped shirt and one bare foot, and he shuffled closer. I was pretty sure having my skirt bunched up around my hips and flashing the creases of my ass didn't help, either. Goddess, I looked a mess.

"Are you hurt?" His hulking frame kept moving closer, sending my heart to gallop in my chest.

"No, wait." My sudden shout stopped him in his tracks. "Stay there, Davon, you don't want to get bitten." Think Hazel, think.

"Bitten? What the hell, Hazel. Get away from there right now. What's in there?" When a gun cocked, I knew the jig was up. If he saw the demon, there was no doubt in my mind I'd be in more trouble than I already was.

"It's a dog, okay. Stay back because if you spook it, it'll bite me. Then I'll be pissed. Do you want that?" Where the hell was my coven?

"What kind of a dog?" Tone dripping with suspicion, his feet scraped the floor as he cautiously moved closer again. If he saw the Kishi starfishing it, not even my grandmother could cover the mess up.

"You are the one with a flashlight, Davon, so why don't you tell me. I'm not playing games when I tell you to stay back. Look at my face." I added an additional scowl for good measure, shuffling on my knees to hide the Kishi sprawled a couple of feet away, deep enough in the shadows not to be visible for the moment.

"What about it?" I could've laughed at the weariness in that loaded question, but he did stop coming closer.

"Does it say approachable to you right now?"

"It never does," he muttered, and I grinned at him like a fiend. "This is crazy. You don't get to boss me around after you dumped me."

"I already parted with my right boot, and I love these boots. You wanna try the left one? I can nail you in the forehead or in the jingleberries. Your choice," I threatened while internally freaking out. Being a bitch to Davon wouldn't work much longer. It never did. He would do the opposite of what I told him just to spite me. I could feel it.

"Hello," a female voice called from the entrance of the warehouse, and I deflated like a balloon recognizing my best friend Sissily. About freaking time. The demon was dazed, but he wouldn't stay down much longer. And if he woke up with Davon here, I had a nagging feeling my body parts would join those scattered around the warehouse in jars. Courtesy of my grandmother, of course. The demon didn't have shit on her when that witch got pissed.

"Stop right there. Police." Davon pointed his gun and flashlight at Sissily's face. Protecting her poor eyesight with a forearm flung in front of her, she blinked at him as if ready to say something.

"Is this your dog?" I rushed to say before she screwed me over. You never knew what would come out of her mouth. "It might be injured, it almost bit me."

"Hazel ..." Davon started in a warning tone.

"Yeah, oh thank goodness you found him," Sissily

gushed, overdoing it a little, if you asked me. Whatever Davon wanted to say was silenced, thank the goddess.

"If this is your dog, Ma'am, I must report it, I'm afraid. It attacked a civilian, and it's considered dangerous." Davon, the good cop he always was, started reading Sissily her rights while she rolled her eyes.

I sighed, pinching the bridge of my nose.

"Oh, shut up human." Her hand flicked when she had enough of his word vomit, and she zapped him hard enough the poor guy convulsed a long moment before he passed out, the gun and flashlight clattering on the concrete.

Then she turned her blue peepers my way and gave me a once-over. Although her blonde hair was smooth and all in one place, and her pencil suit was sharp enough to cut a finger off, Sissily had no right to grimace at me. Someone should tell her "I bit a rotten lemon" was never a good look on a chick. Just saying.

"If you say a word Im'ma boob punch you." Pushing off the ground, I swayed, and for the second time I failed to glue the ripped silk sleeve together. "Are you alone?" It was improbable, but a girl could hope.

"The others are not far behind me. I had a feeling you'd jump right into this, so I made sure I came before anyone else. What do we have?" She sashayed closer, giving Davon a disgusted look.

"Kishi demon." I glared at the asshole who finally stirred with a groan.

"How do you find yourself in these situations, Hazel?" Ignoring her, I was still messing with the sleeve, so with a sigh, she took her jacket off and handed it to me.

"Thanks." Limping a couple of steps forward, I plucked it from her fingers. "And I wasn't kidding about the boob punch. I'll even twist your nipple until you scream if you don't keep your voice down."

"You do know we're not five anymore, right?"

"What's your point?"

I could tell she had so much to say just by the tightening of the tendons on her neck. Her throat worked, her mouth opening and closing until she gave up and shook her head.

Yeah, exactly my sentiments.

"Where's your other boot?" She followed the elaborate swirl of my finger until it pointed at the demon. My beautiful, precious boot was sticking out of his throat, covered in black blood and gore. Then she arched an eyebrow, which should've looked stupid on anyone except me, but on Sissily everything looked good. If she wasn't my best friend and if I had magic, I would've hexed her with warts. I hoped the girl knew how lucky she was that I loved her like a sister. What surprised me more was she loved me back the same, even though I was an asshole. At least most of the time.

"I've always told you fashion is a weapon if you learn how to use it. Did you believe me? Of course you didn't." My smirk earned me a twitch of her mouth. If anyone knew Sissily they'd know it for the huge win that was. She never smiled on a job.

"Danika is going to lose her shit." We both shivered at that.

As if saying the name conjured her, my grandmother's power preceded her presence, filling the warehouse with magic and saturating the air with the strong scent of ozone.

"Hazel Byrne." I flinched when my name echoed in the silent building, and Sissily copied me sympathetically. "Show your face this instant." My grandmother swooped in like a hungry vulture honing-in on a roadkill.

Me. I was the roadkill.

Thankfully, the lights came on inside the building, blinding me momentarily as thumps of many feet scattered throughout the warehouse. Our coven mates spread around the vast space like ants. I blinked like an idiot a few times until my vision cleared, and that was when I saw the look on her face. Cold, emerald eyes sharp enough to cut a diamond rolled over me from head to toe, assessing and judging while telling me she found me lacking in many ways. I gulped and tugged Sissily's jacket closer. Then Danika's unreadable gaze fell on Davon, who took a lesson from the Kishi demon and was starfishing it in the middle of the damn place. She stilled at the sight of a human cop and stabbed me with a glare afterwards.

"That was Sissily, not me." The words burst from me so fast I almost spit on my lower lip.

"Snitch," my best friend hissed, but her chin jutted out and she stepped closer to me.

"Every bitch for herself, remember?" I mumbled behind my hand when I raised it to wipe my mouth in case I was still drooling. Those Manhattans were buzzing in my head like a cloud of bees and making my tongue too thick for my mouth while I swayed where I stood. Oh boy was I screwed.

Sissily snorted but coughed to cover it up. Her reaction earned me a disapproving look from my grandmother, which I felt all the way to my soul. The woman saw everything no matter how hard I tried to hide it, and her hearing was better than a vampire's. I didn't have to guess because I *knew* she heard us.

I was the best fighter they had in our coven. Hand-to-hand or weapon combat, I could take them all down, and that included our high priest. But thanks to my lack of magic, I somehow always ended up looked down on, especially by Danika Byrne. Even when I did get the job done.

One demon stabbed in the throat with a designer boot, case and point.

"We will speak back at the coven." With flare, she spun on her heel, her long dress billowing behind her as she stormed out of the warehouse and left me grinding my teeth.

"Let's go." Linking her hand through mine, Sissily tugged me along with her because she probably assumed I would run. And honestly, I thought about it for like two point five seconds. It was pointless since everything I had was in the house I shared with my grandmother, but it sure was tempting. I wobble-limped alongside Sissily, glancing at my coven mates as they packed everything, including the Kishi demon I apprehended.

"She will chill out by the time we get back." My best friend gnawed on her lower lip, not believing her own assurances.

"I don't care." My shrug didn't fool her since I was patting my hair to smooth it and probably looked constipated just thinking about facing my grandmother behind closed doors.

Because Danika Byrnes never chilled. Like ever. My grandmother was born with a stick so far up her ass the goddess herself couldn't find it if she tried.

She was going to hand my ass to me, and I had no other choice but to take whatever she dished out. A sinking suspicion that it would involve cleaning churned in my stomach right beside the booze.

There was a first time for everything, though. She might've grown a heart in the last twelve hours. Or took it from some random jar and shoved it in her chest. My head tilted to the side, I contemplated it for a second.

One look at my grandmother's disappearing form, with

those stiff shoulders and that head held high, killed that hope. There was no escaping a punishment.

With a groan, I followed my best friend into the belly of the beast.

The whole way back to the coven, I kept trying to picture my eyeballs floating in a jar on top of my grandmother's desk.

They were a nice shade of golden honey, if I did say so myself. I'd have them in a jar too if I didn't need them.

Chapter Two

The Gatekeeper's coven was located dab smack in the middle of Cleveland, of all places. The temple walls stretched high toward the sky like the open mouths of baby birds waiting for a worm to fall into their gaping maws. A domed ceiling made of glass, to better see the full moon each month, covered almost half the block. Made out of black stone, the building looked menacing, and the three keys – a symbol representing Hecate- painted in blood red above the tall double doors of the entrance stood out stark against it. Since it was late at night, magical flames were shooting seven feet tall on each side of the stars leading to it, casting it in an eerie-hellish hue. No wonder humans gave us a wide berth.

Pausing at the bottom of the marble steps that would lead me inside, I glanced up and down the street. An urge to book it down the sidewalk and find a place to hide for a day or two was very tempting. However, with only one boot and still mostly drunk, there was no way I could outrun Sissily. She might sympathize with me, but she was a stickler for the rules, and she was smart enough not to want to anger Danika, unlike me. I had no doubt she'd tackle me and drag me kicking and screaming inside by the hair. She did that once in middle school when I didn't want to go back inside with her after lunch break. The humans mulling around would be no help, either. Ever since we came out of the closet, so to speak, they gawked like we were circus freaks but wouldn't come closer than a few feet, as if magic was contagious and they might get infected. I wish it was.

There were exceptions like Davon the cop, but those were few and far between. We were "the others," and unless they needed help, humans wanted nothing to do with us. At least there were no pitchforks or burnings at the stake involved, so not bad I guessed. That was why my coven was very strict. The government told us we were all good to live among humans as long as no problems came up by *any* supernatural being, not just us. So, the high priest and my grandmother—to be honest it was probably all her because the priest was practically a mute when around her—decided we would boss the supernatural world around. The magi police force was just a front for posturing. We were the ones that got down and dirty. And destroyed perfectly new pairs of designer boots in the process, I'd like to add.

Sissily took my elbow and waddled me up the steps when I took too long to move. Chewing on the inside of my mouth, I allowed my fear to choke me until I reached the double doors, and then I squared my shoulders. Whatever issues I had would be left at the door. No one needed to know my shit. It was none of their business, anyway.

The inside of the building was also painted black, with a hallway like one long intestine twisting around offices, ritual rooms, guest reception halls, and the library, of course. Our pride and joy, with knowledge gathered for generation after generation by magical families. It was the largest collection in the world, and the love of my grandmother's life. I personally used it to hide from idiots when they got annoying, or to pretend I was busy when we had a ritual scheduled. If I was busy, I couldn't participate and see all the pitying looks or sneers thrown my way.

"You ready?" Sissily mumbled under her breath and dragged me out of my spinning thoughts.

"No."

"Hazel."

"Why does everyone think saying my name will help anything?" I jerked my elbow out of her pinching hold and tugged hard on the borrowed jacket to straighten it. My balance went sideways, and I pitched forward, but she tugged me back before I face planted. "Let me tell you, it does nothing but piss me off and feed my anxiety. I know what my name is. I've had it my whole life, thank you very much."

"You're stalling."

"No." I gasped dramatically. "What in the world gave you that idea?" Sissily rolled her blue peepers at me. "I really don't want to go in. I might puke all over her desk."

"You're so stupid." She snickered and bumped my shoulder. For her sake, my lips pulled to the side in a pathetic attempt at a smile.

With a sigh, I continued my impersonation of Quasimodo hobbling down the hall on one high-heeled boot and one bare foot, darting glances at the candelabras lining the walls. Black pillar candles burned in clusters with blue flames, the magical fire standing straight without a crackle or a flicker. They always looked like a painting that gave off light to me, and it didn't matter how many times I saw them.

"They are expecting you." We hadn't fully rounded the corner yet, but Mike made sure to shout it like he was playing bingo and just won. He leered at Sissily, but as soon as he met my glare, his head ducked down so fast he almost headbutted the desk.

"I see you didn't take your meds today, Mike?" I jabbed him conversationally, and Sissily snorted.

"What? Yes, I did." His face snapped up and reddened like a tomato. "Hey, I don't take medication."

I pursed my lips, eyeing him and pretending like I didn't believe him.

Something told me if I kept looking at him his head might explode. I was willing to test that theory, but I felt Danika's magic reaching, plus Sissily nudged me to get moving.

"Maybe you should." My suggestion to the creep in passing left him sneering. "Meds won't grow your brain, but it'll help with your complexion."

We left him stuttering and talking to himself about bitches and the goddess knew what other fairy tales he told himself. After he dared to treat my best friend like she was his personal punching bag while she dated him, I made it my business to mess him up every chance I had. I was pretty sure he cast a protection spell around himself specifically against me so I couldn't physically harm him. Good thing, too, because I didn't trust myself not to fillet him like a fish.

I flung the door open without a knock and hobble-hopped inside my grandmother's office with Sissily nipping on my heels. Stopping in my tracks, I took in the large, ornate-oak desk Danika Byrne sat ramrod straight behind. High Priest Shadowblood was behind her right shoulder, his face pinched so tight it looked like he was trying not to fart. His slicked dark hair, long, thin nose, and pointed chin brought the image of a crow perched on my grandmother's shoulder to my mind every time he did that, although I never dared mention it. But it wasn't those two that made me freeze with one foot in the air and one hand gripping the doorknob.

No, it was the third person in the room just to the left of Danika. In his late twenties to mid-thirties, he was a face I'd never seen before between these walls. His blond hair was shaved close to his skull on the sides, with the top left longer to drape over his forehead in a wave. Eyes the color of melted chocolate flicked my way when I opened the door, and they widened in interest—not enough to be obvious, but since I was staring at him like an idiot, I noticed. A square jaw and a nose with a slight bump at the bridge like it had been broken a time or two framed full lips more suitable to a woman than someone like him. Wide shoulders stretched his indigo button-down shirt, which was tucked into the waistband of dark slacks that emphasized his narrow waist and muscular body. I gawked for less than five seconds, but it was enough for one corner of his mouth to twitch. That little quirk snapped me out of my daze.

Spinning around, I bolted out of the office and plowed Sissily down. She would've fallen on her ass if I didn't catch her by the arm and drag her back out with me. The door closed behind us with a loud thump when I bodily carried her to the desk where Mike was still muttering curses at me.

"Give me your shoes." My best friend squeaked when I plopped her ass on the desk.

"What? Why?"

"Shoes woman. Now." My hand was wiggling in her face to show my urgency. "Questions later."

I yanked them off her feet myself because I had no time to explain why having shoes instead of one boot—regardless of how pretty said boot may look—was so important. Lifting her leg up pushed Sissily until she was leaning on her hands, and if I wasn't in a hurry I would've chortled at Mike's face. Poor schmuck almost swallowed his tongue when he received a face full of a ponytail, and his saucer-like eyes told me he didn't miss Sissily's boobs sticking up from her arched back. I even stabbed her foot in my one boot because I was a good friend like that, and then I was yanking her along with me to enter the office for the second time. She'd probably replace my shampoo with glue to pay me back for this, but I'd deal with it later.

When I stepped back inside the office, my grandmother arched an eyebrow not looking very pleased, which I ignored, of course. Being the nice little witch I was, I waited for Sissily to limp inside before I closed the door and guided her to the closest chair. Her blue eyes were spitting daggers at me the whole time. As Sissily dropped on the uncomfortable chair, I went as far as petting her head like a puppy that did potty, ignoring her glare the entire time. Then, I turned and beamed at everyone in the room, giving my grandmother a pointed look towards blondie that said help a girl out but I had a feeling my plea fell on deaf ears.

"Hazel, what happened tonight?" Danika Byrne got down to business, stapling her fingers under her chin and leaning her forearms heavily on the desk. If looks could kill, Sissily would be reading my obituary right now.

Smile frozen on my face to flash my pearly whites, I widened my eyes at her. "What?" My lips didn't move as I pushed the question through my teeth. My best friend groaned from the side.

"What in the goddess's name is wrong with you?" I swore lightning flashed in Danika's emerald eyes. "Are you hurt? Did the demon do anything to you?"

"We don't discuss coven business in front of strangers, Dani—I mean, Ma'am. Grandmother," I added that last bit lamely as an afterthought, and the thunderous expression twisting her features told me she didn't miss it.

"River Blackman is an apprentice of our high priest, Hazel." She looked down her nose at me like I was supposed to be psychic and guess who was who around here without introduction. "There are no strangers."

Wait, what?

"You can have your shoes back." With a groan, I turned to Sissily and started tugging the shoes off my feet. I shoved them in her face, and she recoiled as if I'd thrown snakes at her.

"I don't want them." She attempted to slap my hands away with a mortified look on her face, but I was very persistent when I needed to be.

"Well, you're having them." I jabbed them at her again. "Give me my boot."

"What in the world is going on?" We all ignored the high priest when he mumbled at no one in particular, sounding perplexed.

"You are aware that you are nuts, right?" Sissily muttered under her breath, but she tugged her shoes on, and I yanked the one boot over my foot.

"Of course. I'm an asshole, Sissily, but I'm not stupid." She blinked at my incredulous tone, but I was already turning toward the rest of the people in the room.

A muscle twitched under my grandmother's eye.

"When the call came for the demon, everyone that answered was at least twenty minutes away. Everyone in this room knows they are sneaky and fast." I figured I'd get it over with. "I was closest to the demon, so I answered the call and made sure he didn't escape. Long story short, he is in our hands and the warehouse ransacked ..." Danika's scowl was a creature all on its own. "I'm sure you don't want to hear my internal debate about sacrificing my new boots so he didn't get away, Grandmother."

Grating on my nerves was the fact that River's eyes were dancing with suppressed humor. *Laugh it up, asshole, because I'll make you cry soon enough.* I wasn't sure he read the message I shot his way through my narrowed gaze, but he couldn't say he wasn't warned. Being a dud was a sure thing to get you bullied in a coven full of powerful witches, so instead of dealing with that, I became a master at cracking their noses with my fist. The blondie wouldn't know what hit him.

"I do want to hear every detail there is. Starting with what possessed you to go there in the first place. Fighting a demon without magic is unacceptable." If she noticed my flinch, she didn't show it. "He could've killed the last of the Byrne line, you insolent girl."

"How's this for a recap, Danika?" I snarled. The gasp from Shadowblood sounded scandalized when I slapped both hands on her desk and leaned forward so we were at eye level. "I can kick any demon's ass, including every idiot you have inside this coven, in six-inch heels, without breaking a sweat, and with my arms tied behind my back. I showed up at the warehouse, cracked the demon's head on the concrete like a melon, then I stabbed him with my new boot. Which you owe me a new pair, plus an iPhone, just so you know. Then the rest of you waltzed into posture with your magic and clean up the place. That good enough of an explanation for you?"

"How dare you speak like that?" High Priest Shadowblood stuttered, his neck elongating as he tucked his chin in. "You are not a savage, young lady."

"Aren't I, though?"

"Show respect to your grandmother," he snapped.

"You got one thing right, pops." My empty stare flicked his way, and he took an involuntary step back. *If they don't string me from the roof tonight, I'm honestly never drinking again.* "*My* grandmother, and I'm doing exactly what she taught me. To quote her, 'you treat people the way they treat you.' So, I will talk to her however damn well I please. In this case, I'm showing her the same respect she gave me." I believe Shadowblood was about to have an aneurism.

"Hazel," Danika leaned back in her chair on a sigh, all fight draining out of her. "I wasn't trying to insult you because you have no magic."

For an old witch, barely any lines were visible on her beautiful face. She might be a stick-up-the-ass nag, but no one could dispute the fact she still turned heads. Midnight blue hair spilled around her face like a waterfall, bringing attention to her alabaster skin and piercing emerald eyes. Tall for a woman, she was curvy where it counted, but most admirable of all was her presence. When Danika Byrne walked into a room, you knew it even if your back was turned.

"No, you were complimenting me on a job well done." With one last stare at Shadowblood, I pushed off the desk. "If we are done here, I need a shower. I can smell the Kishi demon on my skin."

"I need you to promise me—"

"I will not step foot anywhere where your precious witches with magic need to go." My smile could cut glass when I looked at her over my shoulder. "I'll just stand back and look pretty."

"You are not replaceable, Miss Byrne—" Shadowblood started, but I cut him off.

"No, I'm to be kept as a broodmare, High Priest Shadowblood. I'm aware." That got the reaction I expected from my grandmother.

"For the next week, you will be cleaning the library, Hazel," Danika snapped and stood to her full height, which was a couple of inches higher than mine. She did it on purpose so I had to look up at her. *Nice power play, Grandma.* "And the ritual room, too, until I say that you are done. Am I clear?"

"Crystal." I dared a glance at River, but with his hands clasped at the small of his back, he was frowning at his boots. *Welcome to the Gatekeeper's Coven, blondie, this is how we treat family.* The guy hasn't done anything to me, but just seeing him standing behind that desk with Danika and Shadowblood put him in my shit bucket, too.

"Let's go," I called out to my best friend, who was in the office for moral support more than anything else.

We almost made it out the door. Almost.

"Sissily, you'll join Hazel in her tasks." My grandmother was already back in her chair and had turned to say something to River Blackman, a blunt dismissal of us if ever I saw one.

We spilled out of the office without another word. "Why do I pay every time you get into trouble, little jerk?"

"Because you are the only one that can call me that and live, big jerk." I threaded my arm through hers, leaning against her for support.

"True." She sighed and placed her head on my shoulder. "On a good note, not even you can get in trouble inside a library."

Lesson 2: *Never tempt fate.*

That bitch bit.

Chapter Three

"Hazel?"

Sissily's tone was low when she hissed my name, but in the silence of the library, it boomed like a gun going off next to my ear. My head jerked up for no reason at all since I knew she'd be coming to join me. The back of my skull connected with the thick wooden shelf above me with a dull heavy thud, which made dark roses bloom at the corners of my eyes as I crawled backward, extracting myself from my hidey hole. I had no doubt my best friend had a perfect view of my ass sticking up in the air while I wiggled my way out, but my glare made sure any comment she had stayed behind her closed mouth.

Her lips stayed pressed closed for exactly thirty seconds. Tops.

"I still don't understand why you had to take my shoes," Sissily grumbled under her breath, still stuck on the same thing two days later as she handed me a stack of ancient texts we had to catalogue. Courtesy of the Kishi demon I nailed with my poor ankle boot.

"That should be your answer." Her elbow connected with my side, forcing me to grunt. Exasperated, I huffed, shaking the books in my hands at her face. "You can't understand why you would need to leave a good first impression because you have magic, woman. That's all a guy in our world needs to feel and he gets the googly eyes. I, on the other hand, don't have magic. Apart from the respect I receive around here …"

"That's not respect, Hazel. They're afraid of you. There is a difference," she told me so calmly you'd think she just gave me a compliment.

"That's beside the point. As I was saying, I only have the respect, so I have to make a good impression with my sense of style, too." We both knew I was talking smack. If I stopped doing that, I would have to curl up in a ball and start rocking back and forth.

"I still don't get the shoes."

"Hecate help me, would you stop with the damned shoes? I didn't want to limp on one boot like a dumbass in front of a hottie, okay? How was I to know blondie was one of Grandmother's pawns?" Admitting my vanity was never easy, although she knew me better than I knew myself.

"He is easy on the eyes, I'll give you that." A smile ghosted her mouth, and she bumped me with her shoulder while tucking a loose strand of hair behind her ear.

"Great. Have at it because he is all yours. In the meantime, grab that stack of books over there." Pointing my chin at the pile ready to tip over, I pushed the last book in my hands on the shelf between two others.

In a normal life, when someone told you that you'd be cleaning a library, you'd expect rows of books lining the walls and pretty tables with single little lamps where people could read in peace and quiet. Since nothing was as it should be in this place, half of the vast room was packed with jars full of floating eyeballs, teeth, fingers, or other body parts I tried very hard not to pay too close attention to. A shiver raked my spine, and my friend noticed.

"Ignore those, I'll fix them up." Sissily allowed me to keep my dignity because we both knew I'd end up begging her to do it so I didn't have to touch them. "I honestly don't know why you insist that everyone thinks you are this mean little shit when you have a heart of gold." She shuffled back to me with an armful of tomes, not missing my grimace. "You can say whatever you want, but I know you."

"I should kill you so you keep my secret, then." I snatched the books, turning my back so she didn't see the tears that prickled the back of my eyes.

"Do try, I'm begging you," my friend purred, cocking her hip.

Sissily was the strongest witch in our coven after Danika and Shadowblood. She had every right to be cocky, and for the life of me, up to this day, I couldn't tell why she chose me to be best friends with. By doing that, she made sure her name was whispered behind our backs by all the petty witches in our community, too. A fact that rubbed me wrong on so many levels and made me bare my teeth at everyone, while she couldn't care less about the gossip mill. Regardless of what she said, it was her with the heart of gold, taking strays—or duds as it was in my case—under her protection. Coven mates tried using their magic against me at the beginning, knowing I couldn't fight back the same way, until she unleashed ropes of fire and sent a few of them to the infirmary with third-degree burns. Danika was ready to peel the skin off her bones until she walked in and saw us with arms wrapped around each other, jutting our chins at her in defiance. After a long, loaded look, my grandmother's mouth twitched at the edges and she walked away without a word. We were four at the time, and since that day, we'd been glued at the hip. Unfortunately for my friend, that meant she got in a lot of trouble because of me. I had no magic, but I had fists.

"Do I look dumb to you?" I pointed at myself. "I didn't think so."

Sissily giggled and walked to the floor-to-ceiling shelves full of jars across from where I was standing. "How much longer do you think she will hold us here?" In jeans, a t-shirt, and with her hair in a ponytail, she looked comfy, unlike me in my skirt and blouse.

"I don't know," I answered honestly with a sigh. "If I kept my mouth shut, we may have gone without punishment, but I just couldn't let that go. I swear sometimes I think Danika says things on purpose because she knows I'll react. If I didn't know better, I'd say she rubs salt in an open wound when she needs both of us out of her way."

"What do you mean?" Sissily twisted toward me, hugging a jar full of imp fingers to her chest.

I sawed my teeth over my lower lip, contemplating if I should voice my thoughts or keep my mouth shut. When her blue eyes narrowed on me, I knew I better speak up or she'd never let it go. My best friend was as stubborn as a mule.

"She knows that not having magic is a sore subject for me." Eyes darting around to make sure no one was around, I took a couple of steps closer to her, keeping my tone low. "It's a sore subject for her, too, since I've heard her raging about idiots and how they didn't value their lives because they treated me like I was nothing. So why else would she slap my lack of magic in my face unless she wanted me punished and out of her way?"

I could almost hear the gears turning in Sissily's head. The corners of her mouth slanted slightly down, and the edges of her eyes narrowed. She had her thinking face on while her eyes searched mine.

"Every time I'm punished, you are in the same boat, too ..." I trailed off.

"In the last seven to eight months, more so than ever." Sissily nodded, the jars completely forgotten.

"Well, now that you mention it, yeah." Frowning, I ignored the unease swirling inside me. Witches came to their full potential of power at the age of twenty-three, which for both of us was a few years ago. My best friend and I had our birthdays three days apart, and we were both twenty-six now, so that couldn't be the reason for Danika tucking us away more often than usual. "I can't think of a reason—"

"I can." Plonking the jar with a loud thump, Sissily snatched my hand and dragged me deeper between the rows of books. "About nine months ago, the other covens called a meeting in Atlanta. Do you remember?" She waited for my head to dip in confirmation before continuing. "According to Mike—"

"You still talk to that douchebag?" My mouth closed shut with a snap when she shot me a glare.

"The other covens pressured Danika to reassess the contributions of her coven because it's not fair"—She used air quotes and twisted her mouth— "for most of the Gate-keeper's Coven to be in power. Apparently, they had witches in their ranks, which would be a better fit for enforcers. I think the new guy is here for that reason, by the way."

"And I jumped in to apprehend a Kishi demon with no magic at all." With a groan, I buried my face in both hands, ignoring the comment about River.

"Yeah." Her nails dug into my forearm where she was still holding onto me. "So, if what you have noticed is true, I will bet my magic it has something to do with that."

"There you are, Hazel." The words died on my tongue, and I spun around to face the witch smirking at us from the other end of the shelves. I wanted to tell Sissily what I said was only a suspicion gnawing at me and not facts, but it'd have to wait.

"Is there a reason you are breathing the same air as me?" I asked Sasha Airborne, nemesis number one from our coven. Sissily clutching my arm made it look like she was holding me so I didn't jump the witch, which worked in my favor.

She took a step back before catching herself.

"The crescent moon chamber needs to be cleaned for the midnight ritual." Her drawled words made me grind my teeth, and Sissily clamped her fingers harder on my forearm. "The High Priest Shadowblood said you need to do it stat. So chop-chop, get to it."

"Hazel …" Sissily hissed, but I shook her off and was already striding to Sasha.

The witch didn't have time to bolt before I stood in front of her and grabbed a fistful of her shirt, twisting it in my grip to bring us nose to nose. She could've been beautiful with her flame-red hair and sky-blue eyes, if she wasn't a snake.

"Last time I checked, Shadowblood is perfectly capable of speaking for himself. Why are you here?" My crazy eyes reflected back at me in her wide-eyed gaze. This close, I'd knock her ass out before she had time to call on her magic, and we both knew it.

When the warmth of magical flames washed over my back, I knew Sasha was debating whether or not to take a chance, especially since Sissily stood behind me giving her a light show with her fire magic. Venom burned in Sasha's eyes, and she answered through clenched teeth.

"I told him I was coming this way and I'd pass the message along."

"You didn't learn your lesson last time you decided to pick on someone stronger than you?" Her skin paled, telling me she remembered the time when she decided it'd be fun to corner me with her friends and they cut my face and arms using air magic. They had me pinned like a bug on the wall and chortled like it was all fun and games. For them, it might've been. I had a different opinion on the matter.

That memory was burned in my brain along with the crippling pain of feeling my skin splitting open and the grating sound of their laughter while I begged them to stop. It was one of the few times Sissily was not with me, and they took full advantage of that. We were eleven. I couldn't remember much of how things played out after that, just that I came out of the daze on my knees with Sasha and her friends beaten to a bloody pulp around me. Something dark and hungry swirled in my chest when I thought about it, whispering in the back of my mind that I should make her suffer.

"Everything okay here, ladies?"

I released Sasha at the sound of the smooth baritone that washed over us like a balm. She stumbled away from me, throwing a glare over her shoulder as she darted out of the library and shouldered out right past River Blackman. Before I could grab her, Sissily bolted too, turning my way only after she was behind River, grinning like a fool and giving me a thumbs up.

Like a somersault, my stomach dipped when his raspy

chuckle filled the library and he stepped inside. My shoulders hunched as if preparing me to run for the door, which was stupid on so many levels, but he closed the heavy door with a thud that held some finality to it.

Goosebumps popped up over my arms when I met his brown eyes and saw the intensity there.

"I don't believe we were properly introduced." Blondie swaggered closer until I could feel the warmth of his nearness through my clothes. "I'm River."

"Hecate cursed me." As soon as I realized I spoke out loud, my gaze snapped up to meet his.

"I'd say it made you quirky and very intriguing, Miss Byrne." A smile ghosted over his full mouth before it turned into a panty-melting grin. "I won't say cursed, unless that's what you make of it, of course."

Why did he have to be buddies with Shadowblood and my grandmother? Why?

Chapter Four

"Unless you need a book, an eyeball or, let me guess …" Tapping a finger on my lip, I pretended to think about it before snapping my fingers in River's face. "A dried-up minotaur testicle, maybe?" The revulsion washing over his features was priceless. "Unless you need one of those, I suggest you get the hell out of my way, pretty boy."

Blondie stilled when I was done talking, and after a long moment full of pregnant silence, I turned my back on him. My mind was still spinning from Sissily's reminder of the coven meeting more than half a year ago. I never claimed to be well behaved or a good person, but the number of times I'd been tucked away in the library or busy with any other task Danika dumped on my head lately did break the record. Almost as if she did everything in her power to keep me out of everyone's sight. Out of sight, out of mind type of thing.

Through the years, I somewhat learned how to push away all thought of being useless to my coven, as well as my family—more so the Byrne bloodline than any others—

going so far as to even convince myself that I didn't care what anyone thought of me. It was a lie, and we could lie to ourselves better than anyone else, which made me a perfect example for it. I actually believed it, too, until something popped up to trigger the soul-wrenching pain I had buried so deep I nearly forgot it was there. But I remembered it now.

Oh, how I remembered.

Absent-mindedly, I returned to tucking away the rest of the ancient texts that waited for me, my fist rubbing at the dull ache at the center of my chest. My grandmother raised me the best she knew how. I couldn't begrudge her the tough love she bestowed upon me since in a way it had prepared me for the harsh life outside our family home. Did I like it? No, definitely not. Did I appreciate it? Thinking back on all the torment and cruel words spat my way, I had to admit that I was grateful to her. Just occasionally, however, I wished I'd grown up with someone loving me even when I screwed up. Even though I had no magic in my blood.

Like I was good enough just because someone had me in his or her life.

Going through the motions without being aware of what I was doing, I nearly jumped out of my skin when River cleared his throat behind me. I forgot he was standing there like a statue a few feet from the door.

"Are you okay, Miss Byrne?" The low tone of his voice made it seem like he genuinely cared, and the way his gaze searched my face only twisted the ache inside me until I was scared it might double me over.

"What kind of a dumb question is that, Mr. Blackman?" Looking down my nose at him over my shoulder, I said his name mockingly. "Of course, I am fine. About those testicles though ..."

"I don't need testicles." His jaw clenched, and his eyes narrowed on me.

The asshole that I am, I dropped my gaze to his crotch, giving it a skeptical once-over. "I dunno ..." When a muscle started dancing on one side of his face, I shrugged. "Suit yourself, just don't say I didn't offer."

"I see," River purred so close behind when I gave him my back again, his breath tickling the short hairs on my neck.

"You see nothing." Hoping my dismissive, toneless words would send him on his way, I stepped sideways to get away from him.

"Yet you still think I'm pretty," he jabbed, and my head snapped in his direction to find him watching me with an expression that said he knew something I didn't.

"Whoever sold you that lie should give you your money back."

"You." That stupid smile on his face would crack my molars if he didn't wipe it off soon.

"What about me?" If River had a bit of a brain, he would see the warning in my glare.

"You sold me the lie." The light coming in sheets through the domed roof and floor-to-ceiling arched windows made his blonde hair glow like gold on top of his head when he folded his arms and leaned a shoulder on the bookshelf.

His black button-down shirt stretched over his shoulders and biceps, creasing at the elbows, and the cufflinks he had blinked at me. The flame etched on them announced to any witch he had fire magic and was proud of it since it was openly displayed like that, unlike a lot of others who kept their powers hidden to make those that want to cross them wonder about it. Pretty arrogant, if you asked me, but I was jealous so no one should take my word for it. His dress pants had sharp lines in the middle of his strong legs the fabric couldn't hide, falling over loafers shined to a point you could use them as a mirror. If I didn't know him for the snake in the grass he was, I would need to rub my eyes to make sure I wasn't dreaming and he was indeed real. The goddess didn't shy away when gifting him in the looks department, pouring them in with a ladle. She used a fork with me and I was happy with that. I knew how to work with what I had.

"I'm a pro at lying." Realizing I'd stared way too long, my face warmed up and I turned away from his knowing gaze. "But that lie was free since you looked pathetic when you walked in, so no money back."

"I see that, too." River chuckled, and the melted chocolate of his irises lightened to warm brown in the sunlight.

"You sound like a parrot, and I'm bored, so how about you go bother someone else, huh? I'm busy."

If Sissily and I were right about something going on behind our backs that involved the other covens, River was deep to his eyeballs in it, no matter how enticing those said eyeballs were. Dropping my guard around a pretty face had never seemed more dangerous than at that moment.

"I didn't mean to upset you, Hazel." Pushing off the shelf, he straightened, all humor vanishing from him. I stiffened, expecting him to reach for me. "I just wanted to introduce myself the way I thought it should've been done in the first place. Unfortunately, my arrival in your coven had bad timing."

I could tell he was fighting the urge to touch me when his right hand fisted at his side. Catching myself eyeing him warily sent a fresh wave of anger through me. River Blackman's presence unsettled me in more ways than one, and I didn't like that one bit. I would've been all for playing a game of cat and mouse if he'd picked any other time. Right now, when I could feel the storm brewing just around the corner, when it was ready to unleash on my life like a tornado, my patience was wearing thin no matter how wobbly my knees got around him. He was the most beautiful man I'd ever seen, but I valued my life more than beauty by miles.

If anyone were to check my record so far, I was nothing if not a survivor.

"So you did. Congratulations on that great achievement. Now, if you would kindly leave me alone, I'd like to return to my task, thank you." The vise around my lungs contracted as I watched him debate whether he should say more or not, but reason won in the end. With a small nod, he turned and strode toward the door. "And that's Miss Byrne to you, not Hazel. Familiarity is reserved for friends and family only," I called at his back and didn't need to see him to know he was staring at me.

I felt the weight of his gaze pressing on my shoulders like a mountain being dumped there. After a while, the click of the door closing surrounded me, and releasing a sigh, I leaned my forehead on the dusty books sitting mutely on the shelves. Taking one deep breath after another, I kept my eyes closed until the galloping in my chest slowed to a steady thump. If I was going to get out of whatever was going on, I needed to be on my best game and not allow my hormones to put me off kilter.

When Sissily returned, she found me like that.

"What happened?" My friend rubbed my shoulder in comfort, provoking a smile from me. Leave it to her to sense my turmoil without me saying a word.

"Nothing. I was just thinking about what we talked about before we were rudely interrupted." A change of subject was in order, so I gave her a side-eyed glance. "Should I assume you let Sasha get away or …"

"That idiot will end up forcing my hand one day to kill her, I swear." As I expected, Sissily's attention turned toward our mutual pain-in-the-butt coven mate. With jerky movements, she tugged the elastic band from her hair so she could retie her ponytail. "You should've seen her run down the hall, all the while glancing over her shoulder like I have nothing better to do than chase her dumb ass."

"You are scary when you get pissed off." Snickering at the mocking glare she threw my way, I raised both hands in surrender. "I'm just saying. I wouldn't want to cross your path when you get that look on your face."

"What look? You are mistaking me with yourself. I don't have a look." Done with her hair, she dramatically flicked her ponytail over her shoulder. "I'm as sweet as they come." Which was not far from the truth, and many had made the mistake of judging her by her doll-like exterior, expecting a lamb to only find a ferocious wolf instead.

"Anywho … back to what we spoke about. I have every intention of digging into it." Stomach dipping low, I wiped my all-of-a-sudden clammy hands on my shirt. "If something is about to hit me, I'd rather see it coming."

"We will be digging into it." Sissily flicked a finger between us. "This is a two-woman job, and they've never hidden anything from us for long before. We got this."

"Right. Let's finish this up so we can clean up the ritual room first." Just thinking about it made me grind my teeth. Danika knew how much I hated doing that, and that was why she made me.

Sissily was already grabbing books by the armful and

shoving them haphazardly wherever she found space. I almost laughed at the idea of someone coming to find incantations and ending up with a demon summoning circle. I didn't say anything though, just followed her lead and stuffed texts wherever I could place them.

"And don't think I'll forget about River and what happened here," my friend informed me evenly. "I want to know every word he said, while we are scrubbing gore from floors." She shivered, and I burst out laughing.

"Nothing really, apart from just coming here to take up space for no reason."

"Well, he did look like you kicked his puppy when I passed him in the hallway." She was staring at the books in her hands, but I could tell she was watching me like a hawk. A sensation I didn't want to examine too closely stirred inside me, and I stomped on it before it grew to the point I had to acknowledge it. I didn't answer my friend, instead pretending I was hurrying to finish up, lining the ancient texts. Her noncommittal hum spoke volumes, though. Sissily was a glass half full type of a person, unlike me. I just dumped whatever was in it and crushed the glass under my foot. She wouldn't understand, even if I tried to explain it.

River Blackman was the enemy.

He just didn't know it yet.

Chapter Five

I was tired to my bone marrow when I finally dragged myself home. The keys dangled in my fingers, and it took great effort to lock the car as I climbed up the few stairs leading to the wrap-around porch of my house. Well, Danika's house, where I sort of existed, much like a piece of furniture placed in a corner that you know was there but you rarely looked at it. Just how I liked it. She was under the impression it was too dangerous for me to live alone, and after a few attacks, I agreed.

Now we just were.

My grandmother minded her own business, and I did the same.

Match made in heaven.

The front door loomed in front of me, inviting and promising a warm bed where I could curl up and rest my aching muscles. Its proximity gave me a boost of energy I didn't know I had, and I almost tripped in my haste to get to it when Davon spoke from the path behind me.

"Hazel, do you have a minute?" By the time I managed

to turn, he was already standing at the bottom of the stairs with his head tilted up to lock eyes with me.

Lesson 3: *Never tell a guy where you live so you don't have to deal with stupid shit.*

"No, I don't, but I can tell that won't stop you from speaking your piece, so let's get on with it." The human didn't miss my wince when I shuffled to the side and leaned on the railing.

"Are you okay?" Whatever else he was about to say trailed off when my hand slammed the air between us.

"Stop right there. This is not a social visit, so move to the important stuff, mkay?" Davon seemed put out, but I couldn't care less.

The moment he told me I should just register myself as a human instead of a witch since I had no magic, and when he laughed about my explanation why I couldn't, we were done. There was nothing to say anymore. He should've left it at that. Not that Davon was a bad guy, per se. The cop was nicely built with a swimmer's body, and he had a handsome face to match. The dark waves of his hair were cut military-style short, and the shadow darkening his square jaw complimented the light blue of his eyes. He just couldn't understand why I was stuck in my own world and couldn't all of a sudden jump ship and decide I was a human.

What he didn't know, and never would, was the fact that I actually considered it and went as far as suggesting it to my grandmother. My humble offer was received as well as an ex you wanted to murder showing up at your wedding reception just when you were about to seal the union with a kiss. Danika was also kind enough to tell me that, until that moment, she never thought I'd be the ruin of our bloodline, magic or not. It still smarted just remembering the disappointment on her face and in the tone of her voice. All that was not Davon's fault, but I was hurting and needed someone to blame. He drew the short end of the stick since it was his idea in the first place.

"What exactly happened in that warehouse a couple of days ago, Hazel?" The worried glint in his gaze was replaced with detached coldness, which would've bothered me once upon a time, but not anymore.

"I was drunk and chased a dog to the warehouse. It turns out it was a raccoon, go figure." A sharp pain cramped the muscles of my shoulders when I tried to shrug. I'd never scrub melted wax from altars again, even if Danika killed me. That shit did not come off, and I had a broken nail and chipped nail polish to prove it.

"You are lying." Davon bared his teeth at me in annoyance, telling me that this conversation would not be ending soon.

On a heavy sigh, I dragged myself to the swing on the porch because I needed to sit, or I'd keel over. Those were my only options. Soft cushions cradled me when I plopped on it, the swing rocking back and forth from my weight as I watched Davon come up the stairs to join me. It brought back a memory when we used to sit in this same spot with me curled on his chest and his arms wrapped around me while the air around us filled with the scent of herbs and night blooming jasmine. Everything was the same, only the two of us were different.

"First, I'd think twice before calling me a liar." He didn't join me on the swing, opting to lean his butt on the railing, and I didn't invite him. "Second, I'd go with what I just told you because you are not going to get a different answer. Not now, not ever."

The house was silent and dark, all four stories looming over us. Danika must've stayed late in the coven, and Davon was ruining my chances of escaping her by staring at me through narrowed eyes. Stupidly, I shared a few things with him that I shouldn't have, and this was what I got in return. A human cop interrogating me in front of my damn house.

"Today is the first day I actually know what I'm doing, Hazel," Davon hissed at me. "Two days. Two fucking days are missing from my memories."

I flinched at the venom in his tone.

It slipped once that some witches could alter memories when we had random conversations while enjoying each other's company. As I'd always said, Davon was a good cop, and he paid attention to things that would never cross my mind. He was attentive, and I knew it'd bite me in the ass eventually. I had to get him off my porch before my grandmother showed up, otherwise he might be missing more than two days.

"Have you ever known me to lie to you so I could manipulate you or harm you in any way?"

"You mean apart from the bullshit you fed me when you dumped me?" He looked sinister when he pushed off the railing with the lamps illuminating him at his back and hiding his features. He was just a dark shadow staring down at my upturned face. I said nothing until he snorted and shook his head. "No, I don't think you'd lie just to be malicious."

"Let this one go, Davon. You were at the wrong place at the wrong time. Just know that the problem was solved, and no innocents were hurt in the process," I rushed to add the last part when he sucked in a breath to argue, no doubt.

"Nothing good will come out of it if you keep poking, trust me."

"I don't remember no one being hurt. You seemed banged up pretty good."

"Yeah, well, someone should tell the almighty alcohol that it does not make a witch invincible." My attempt to lighten the mood failed a miserable death. "I've had worse, and as I said, it all ended well. Know that, and just leave it. You, more than anyone, know humans steer clear of witch business. I don't need to lecture you there. Go home, Davon. I need a shower and sleep. I'm not good company tonight."

He followed me step for step as I wobbled to the door, my legs screaming at me to lay down and stretch. It took three tries to get the key in the lock, and just as I turned it, I felt the prickle of the wards wash over me like a breeze. It could've been a clean escape knowing Davon couldn't follow me in even if he tried because the wards would turn him to ash, but the car stopping in the circular driveway messed that up. I fought the urge to scrub a hand over my face so I didn't smear my makeup, and slowly turned to face my grandmother, whose voice was drifting like a murmur to my ears.

"Just say I wasn't picking up and you wanted to beg to get back together ..." I started saying to Davon, but when my gaze landed on the person leaning on the open door of the limo dropping Danika off, the words abruptly stopped.

River was facing my grandmother, but his nonchalant pose wouldn't fool an idiot. His shoulders were stiff, and every muscle on his body was poised like he was expecting an attack. Danika was telling him something, but even she noticed judging by the line forming between her brows on her otherwise smooth face. Blackman was paying attention to her words, but his eyes flickered toward the house one too many times to be considered polite, at least when my grandmother was standing there. At the same time, Davon, seeing where my focus was centered, straightened to his full height and squared his shoulders. Both him and River were over six feet tall, give or take an inch, which dwarfed my five nine unless I wore heels.

For some dumb reason, I grabbed Davon's forearm and yanked him to me, giving him a bone crushing hug. The familiar scent of his cologne—musk with citrusy notes—filled my nose, and it reminded me of all the times I thought he was the answer to end all my torment. Guilt stabbed me because just like then, I used him to hide from things I didn't want to see or feel. It said nothing nice about me, but I still wrapped my arms around his neck when he stiffened. After a moment, I felt him relax and hug me back, his face tucking in my hair.

It was cruel to do this. I knew it, but it didn't stop me from glancing over Davon's shoulder at River. Blondie abandoned any pretense that he was listening to Danika, and he was bluntly staring at me the same way my grandmother was. Unlike her pissed-off glare, he had determination plastered all over his face.

"I'm guessing we are pissing off the dude?" As I said, Davon was too perceptive for his own good.

"Nope." After the "p" popped through my lips, I tried to pull back. "Danika."

"If you say so, Hazel." Davon chuckled and released his hold on me, stepping to the side to allow me to face the vultures walking our way. I guess River was coming in, after all. "And this conversation is not over."

My stomach flip flopped and plummeted to my feet.

"Ms. Byrne." Davon inclined his head when my grandmother glided onto the porch with River at her side.

"Davon, was it?" Danika's intent stare drilled holes in my head before slowly turning on the human.

"It still is," I muttered under my breath, which earned me a look that promised a lot of scrubbing for me.

"Davon, yes." The cop glanced between Danika and River before he stuck his hand at blondie as an afterthought.

"River Blackman." I watched their biceps bunch in their attempts to crush each other's hand. At least Danika's expression changed, taking on amusement instead of anger, but I'd had enough.

"Davon was just leaving." My announcement was a lil' bit louder than I wanted.

The silence that followed was heavy with unspoken words, but eventually the two men released their grips on each other, then Davon leaned down to kiss my cheek before disappearing from the porch with his head held high. When it was just the three of us there, I had to fight my flight instinct so I didn't run to my room like a little girl. My grandmother gave me an unexpected opening when she spoke.

"I hope this has nothing to do with the Kishi demon from the other day."

"That's why I called him." The lie fell easily from my lips. "I wanted to make sure everything was covered. He doesn't remember anything."

"He had two days to report something amiss if he remembered." River, ever the helpful, pointed out the hole in my story.

"Davon would never report anything that could come back to hurt me." I wanted to piss River off, but I knew those words to be true, too. No matter the differences between us, Davon was a good man. One I didn't deserve then, nor now. Not with all the shit going sideways in my life. "I still wanted to make sure he was okay." Which I should've done instead of him seeking me out.

"He did seem to have a soft spot for you, Miss Byrne." River's tone was chilling as his breath whistled through his clenched teeth.

Danika raised an eyebrow but didn't comment.

What was this guy's problem anyway?

"I assure you, Mr. Blackman, my granddaughter does not associate with humans that way."

At the flat way Danika said that, everything me and Sissily discussed hit me like a brick to the head. Instead of trying to show blondie I was off limits by hugging Davon like an idiot, I should've remembered he could be a spy sent from another coven to bring Danika down. If I screwed up by acting like an immature idiot, I'd never forgive myself.

"Davon is just a friend." Swallowing the bile rising from telling another lie, I jutted my chin up. "Plus, he is a good source of information if the coven needs it, not that it's any of your business." Turning away from him, I used a very Danika-like behavior to dismiss him. "I'm glad you are home, Grandmother. I'm very tired, and now that I know you are safe, I can sleep without worry."

River stood stunned and mute when I hugged Danika, which no doubt shocked her too. With one barely there nod aimed his way, I left them on the porch and bolted inside. It was tempting to lurk like a creep and eavesdrop, but I had no energy left in me to do it. I fell asleep soon after I heard my grandmother close her bedroom door with a soft click.

Murder of crows chased me all hours till dawn, trying their best to claw my eyes out. I kept running through the dull gray landscape, barefoot and dressed in a flimsy white dress, until I woke up with a jolt, sitting up in bed drenched in cold sweat. We were taught from a young age that dreams were messages from behind the veil. Whatever the message was, I knew it meant nothing good for me. One thought stayed long after I pulled myself out of the night terror. Someone or something was attempting to prevent me from seeing the truth. The crows were adamant about taking my sight.

It only made me more determined to discover what secrets were hidden from me.

Chapter Six

"I can't believe we found nothing." Sissily chugged her latte like a woman dying of thirst.

It was her fifth one.

Dark smudges sat like war paint under her eyes, and her usually smooth ponytail was sitting askew on the side of her head. The wrinkled t-shirt and leggings just added to the whole disheveled thing she had going on. Just her eyes burned in anger, the blue irises sparkling feverishly under her thick lashes.

I looked just as crazed as her, only I gulped double espresso shots instead of lattes.

Mirrors and hair brushes were distant memories for both of us.

"Maybe there was nothing to find?" Not even I believed that.

The last few weeks we'd combed through everything we could find in the coven and inside my house. If there was something going on, I was sure we would find it in one of those two places, but all our searching confirmed that I was just paranoid. My paranoia rubbed off on Sissily, too, because she was obsessed with finding the foul play. On top of all that, I had to pull medal-worthy maneuvers to avoid River Blackman like the plague, which was not easy at all.

"We are missing something that's staring us in the face. I can feel it." My best friend tilted her cup up before frowning at it when she realized it was empty. She proceeded to shove it at my face and wiggle it, silently asking for another one.

My next breath was blown at her through pursed lips while I replaced her empty coffee cup with a full one I plucked from the cupholder. We'd barely slept since the whole search started, so at the local coffee shop now they plonked three cup holders full of lattes and double espressos in front of us as soon as we walked through their door. I would've given up a while back if our punishments hadn't increased in frequency, Danika going as far as to make me scrub hallways for things I'd done when I was eight. The more she hid me away, the louder the alarms in my head blared.

"Oops." Sissily slurred some words that sounded like curses when an electric current zapped between her fingertips and the coffee cup. Being sleep deprived made the control she had on her magic iffy, and that was the second time she tried to fry an inanimate object.

I was next in line to end up crisp, I could feel it.

The paper cup didn't burn, but steam was curling from the previously cold coffee. After moving it to the side, I placed a Danish in her hand and brought it to her mouth. "Eat before you announce to everyone here what we are."

The owner of the café was a lady from the local pack of shifters, but just because she wasn't human didn't mean she'd be happy if magic started hurling through her shop. Supernaturals had each other's back most of the time, unless it hit their pockets. No comradery could change the fact that the humans had larger numbers and had no problem spending their money in our businesses. Hell, they were the biggest supporters of witches, although they liked us the least of all. We were the scary creatures not to be trusted unless they needed a love potion, a tarot reading, or a ghost hunkered in their house.

Cheery chimes bounced across the café when the front door opened, letting in a gust of hot air along with whoever entered. The line at the counter stretching the length of one wall twisted all the way to the bathrooms, so I couldn't see the door, but I felt it wasn't a human that joined the bustle of people filling up the vast space. My eyes, although gritty and stinging from the bright light coming through the wall of windows, didn't blink for long moments. When no one pushed through the throng of people, I dismissed my worry and turned to watch Sassily stuff the Danish in her mouth until she resembled a chipmunk.

"Wis iz gooz," she told me through a mouthful of food. I handed her a napkin while snickering at her antics.

It was fun to watch the always-put-together Sissily when she let loose and forgot to worry about what others thought. We had one day a month just for that, and the tradition had started about ten years ago. Acting like some caveman in the café didn't fall on that day, but both of us were tired enough not to care at that point. Offering my Danish to her, my hand froze in the air between us as a shadow fell over our table, hiding us from the streaming sunlight. The short hairs on my arm prickled from the proximity of the person looming over us, and my lungs tightened painfully in my chest.

"Ladies." The alpha of the local pack of wolves grinned

at our owlish gawking, his deep tenor vibrating my internal organs long after he was done talking.

"Alex, hi." My friend twinkled her fingers, flakes of pastry spraying from her lips.

"There is no better view than watching a woman enjoy food." The alpha chuckled, swirling a free chair backward and straddling it as he joined us. "I wasn't going to bother you until I saw you. I didn't believe Amber when she told me you might be in some trouble." His whole face lit up when he said the name of his wife, the owner of the café we frequented, but the glint disappeared when he leveled us with his two-colored gaze. One blue and one green eye gave him an intent look without adding the weight of the alpha magic to it.

"No trouble, just work." My friend swallowed hastily and twitched a shoulder, while I still struggled to unglue my tongue from the roof of my mouth.

Alex Greywood was not one to mess with if it could be helped. Apart from Danika, of course, everyone with an ounce of brain stayed out of his way. Including the vamps who terrorized the rest of us. According to all the shifters, not just those in his pack, the alpha was a just and kind leader, but his caring and loyalties ended if you didn't trade shapes. He was known for ripping people limb from limb first and asking questions later when you stepped on his toes. My penchant for sticking my nose where it didn't belong earned Sissily and me a very fragile friendship with the pack alpha.

His youngest kid wandered off pack lands a year ago, somehow ending up at my front door in wolf form. What Alex didn't know and I'd never admit to anyone was the fact I thought it was a lost dog, which I then proceeded to put on a leash and walk around the block searching for his owner. Sissily found me five minutes before the alpha, luckily recognizing the child as a shifter. We were both panicking when Alex and Amber joined us, too overjoyed to see their child safe and alive to notice the dark blue sparkly leash I bought for him dangling off his neck. It turned out the kid was the only boy they had among three other female children, meaning we accidently found and protected the future alpha of their pack.

Alex promised to rip the head off anyone if a hair was missing from our heads that day.

Danika was over the moon with that turn of events.

I was still shaking in my designer shoes just thinking about it.

"Try again, kid." The alpha tapped a forefinger on his nose, reminding us he could smell a lie from a mile away.

For a guy that was over one hundred years old, Alpha Greywood could give a young man a run for his money. Frozen somewhere in his mid-thirties, he was a mountain of a man, with strong, harsh features that screamed of violence hidden behind the faded t-shirt clinging to his large frame for dear life and ripped-at-the-knees jeans tucked into shit-kickers. Unlike most of his kind, though, he was clean-shaven, with just a shadow dusting his too-square jaw and a mop of unruly curls dancing on top of his head. Ebony skin made his mismatched eyes constantly glow like lanterns from his face.

"We can't figure out what's wrong while Danika is doing her best to keep us out of sight from anyone and everyone. Well, keep *me* away. Sissily comes as a plus one always," I blurted out, my eyes widening when it hit me what I'd done.

"You think trouble is coming your way?" The shifter magic slammed into me like a punch to the gut, and quite a few sharp intakes of breath told me not many in the café were as human as I previously thought. The protective instinct of an alpha was no joke, even if it was a self-appointed duty he gave himself when it came to us.

The cat was out of the bag.

"That's the thing ..." Picking at the sticker on my paper cup so I could avoid his intent gaze, I couldn't stop the sigh. "We don't know. Apart from my grandmother's attitude toward me, we have nothing else to go on. It's all a guessing game."

"What does this tell you?" Alex Greywood thumped a fist over his solar plexus. Sissily hummed something under her nose, but I ignored her.

"That I had too many espressos and I might have a heart attack?" My voice raised a pitch, and the comment turned into a question.

The alpha narrowed his eyes on me dangerously.

Blowing out a breath, I closed my eyes and breathed deeply. Shoulders slumped, I pushed the hum of voices to the back of my mind and focused on my intuition. It was a guide any witch would follow, but mine was barely a whisper from the lack of magic. It was the main reason I never trusted it, but I was willing to humor him. I didn't expect the stab of fear and the danger alarm to make me rock back on the chair when I did find it. My chair would've toppled over if Alex didn't snatch me by the upper arm to steady me.

"Danger is definitely coming." With great effort, I pushed the words out through numb lips. Sissily stayed silent, but her face looked paler than it already was.

"This is a good thing, little witch." The shifter looked proud like I'd just discovered the Americas.

"Maybe to you. I personally would love it if danger stayed away from me, thank you very much. I have no magic, or did you forget that?" I should buy his son some chew toys or something, because if anyone else talked like that to the alpha, he would be playing dodgeball with their head by now.

I tensed, expecting him to bark at me or something.

Alex threw his head back, and a booming laugh shot out of him.

Sissily and I blinked dumbly at the guffawing shifter.

"A smart predator is a prepared predator, little witch. And you don't need magic to deal with anything life throws at you. I've seen you fight," Alpha Greywood told me when he was done laughing in my face, reminding me of the time I knocked one of his shifters on his ass after he sniffed me. "You lose your life when danger finds you suddenly and catches you from a blind spot. If you expect it, the chances of survival are great."

"I'll keep that in mind."

"My pack lands are always open if either of you find yourself in a tight spot. Same as my entire pack, if you need a hand." Lifting off the chair, he twirled it before tucking it in its place. "I'll let you enjoy your day. When the time comes, you know where to find me."

We watched him walk to the counter and give his wife a heart-stopping kiss, not giving two shits that the café was packed. A few whistled encouragements made Amber blush and duck her head, but Alex grinned and stomped out of the door with arrogant pride. As far as safety nets go, the little chat with the alpha gave me some sort of peace, at least. Before he sat at our table, I wouldn't have thought of going to him for help, but now that door was left wide open should we need it.

"At least we have a backup now." Sissily yawned so wide her jaw popped. "Maybe we should get some sleep. The last thing I need is to fall asleep in the middle of the ritual Saturday night." Fast calculations told me that was two days from now.

"What ritual?"

"The full moon ritual, little jerk." She snorted, shaking her head. "I swear, some days I wonder if you live in a separate world from mine. You are oblivious."

"Excuse me if I had other things to worry about." I sounded grumpy because I was. "Not like I take part in any of those, so why should I care." Yet again, I'd tempted fate. Both our phones lit up, buzzing and cluttering across the table.

Snatching mine, brand new and all shiny, I expected a call to apprehend some idiot threatening to endanger the thin thread of peace we had with the humans. Not in a million years did I think I'd read the long essay glaring at me from the screen. Fingers flying, I closed the message and opened it again, hoping I'd imagined things. But the same words stared me in the face accusingly. Alex said if I expect it, the chances of survival are great.

I disagreed with him.

"All members of Gatekeeper's Coven will participate in the full moon ritual scheduled for Saturday night, including the leader of the coven, Danika Byrne, and High Priest Shadowblood, along with all family members and apprentices. No exception. Be on time and ready to show your contribution, which you will perform in front of a board of witches, representatives of all covens in America. May Hecate guide your way. Blessed Be."

A torrent of explicit words exploded from Sissily while I held the iPhone limply in my fingers. Did Danika plan on hiding me Saturday night? Even the thought of that was dumb because there wasn't a soul that didn't know who I was and what I was to her.

"Maybe training enforcers to physically fight counts for something." My attempt to comfort Sissily was weak. "Right?"

"Of course it does," my friend hissed like it was me trying to downplay my own significance to my coven. "If that's not enough, I'm sure Greywood would be more than happy to add two witches to his ranks. You heard him."

"True." The need to run was making my skin itch. "Let's go home and get some shut eye. Danika always has a plan, so I'm not too worried," I lied again, while Sissily dutifully agreed with me, rounding the table and linking her hand through mine.

"It could've been much worse," my friend mumbled as we left the café, waving at Amber on our way out. "I totally expected some demon, or worse, Sasha Airborne cloning a few of her and staging an attack." My laugh was short and strained.

"I'm planning on sleeping for two days and kicking ass on Saturday night. You should do the same." I slowed when we reached our cars in the packed parking lot behind the café. "You'll be okay to drive?"

"Duh." Sissily wiggled a tall paper cup at me, which I didn't even see her carrying until then.

"Incorrigible." Shoving her toward her car, I snickered as she sashayed to the driver door of her silver Lexus. "Call me when you make up for lost sleep."

"Will do." She ducked inside the vehicle and slammed the door a little too hard.

My smile slipped when my back was to her. I moved mechanically, getting into my Mercedes and mushing the start button with unseeing eyes. This was bad. Like life-altering bad, and I had no choice but to step into the storm and trust it wouldn't rip me apart. The reason I said I would sleep for two days to my best friend was the fact that I had no intention of going home. When I didn't pick up the phone, she would think I was still in dreamland, while I would be deep in the library searching for any spell or incantation that didn't require magic. I had a strong feeling that I would find my salvation there. Because I didn't tell Alex everything my intuition told me.

I hid the feeling of excitement and elation, along with the abyss of darkness that freaked the hell out of me. Especially when the scent of old books and ink filled my nose in the middle of a café while a faint voice whispered, "Come." Hope was a living thing inside me since, and that led me to my next lesson.

Lesson 4: *The moment hope is all you have left, life will squish it like a bug.*

Chapter Seven

Walking up the massive, marbled stairs toward the coven building at eleven in the morning on any day that didn't fall on a sabbath was like showing up at a funeral drunk, dressed in bikinis, and yelling "Opa." Nerves prickled every inch of my body, stretching my skin so tight I worried it'd start ripping at the seams. It still didn't stop me from taking them two at a time while sending pleas to Hecate to give me a break this one time. Sure as hell, my begging to the goddess who'd deprived me of magic would fall on deaf ears no matter what I did or did not do. My head swiveled left and right to ensure no one watched my desperate attempt to save my hide. Funny how survival instincts woke me up better than all the bitter espressos ever could.

Obsidian walls loomed over me as my feet moved so fast the last few steps to the front door that I nearly tripped and headbutted the ornate wood. My palm connected to the door with a loud slap, and the carving of the tree bit into my skin, but at least my face was saved from having the imprint of it for a week. That was me, the one with the bright outlook on life always counting her blessings. Never mind those were very few and very far between.

Cracking the door open just wide enough to squeeze my butt through it did not help me get rid of the ants crawling over my nerves. There was a persistent itch between my shoulder blades I was dying to scratch, although I knew it wouldn't help even if I clawed at it. The shit load of caffeine didn't help calm my paranoia either, but it did keep my eyes open.

Stepping inside the coven building was like walking into a mausoleum in an ancient and long-forgotten cemetery. A bitter chill in the air nipped at my exposed skin from the lack of magical flames, which left the black pillar candles looking more like hacked-off stumps reaching for the glass ceiling. Dull light bathed everything in gray hues through the silver dome above my head. Contrary to popular belief, witches were not day-loving nutjobs. That stupidity was left to the humans, and thank the goddess for that. A morning person, I was not. Case and point, the coffee replacing the blood in my veins for two weeks. We were just as nocturnal as the vamps. Maybe more so, taking into consideration we followed the power of the moon just as much as her phases. Strong magic or not, there was not a witch in the world who didn't dread the lack of moonlight, which was one reason we controlled the weather like our lives depended on it. Well, not my life since I was screwed either way. The rest of them though …

A nervous snicker shook my shoulders, which I cut short when the sound boomed across the vast space and an echo creepy enough to send a shiver down my vertebrae came back at me. My jutted hip smacked the door closed, and I darted to the closest statue of a robed figure to my left, tucking myself in the stone folds of the robe in case someone heard me. The rock sentinel, her hands pressed together in prayer, stood at nine feet tall and a couple of feet wide, offering protection from prying eyes. If I knew I'd be coming here, I would've taken it easy on the coffee instead of being a jittery mess twitching in my peep-toes and hugging a statue for dear life.

When no one came running to zap me to smithereens for daring to disturb the peace, I poked my head out just to double check. With the coast clear, I tiptoed down the hall while holding my breath because my heart was making a solid attempt at beating right out of my chest. Aware that there were a handful of administration members mulling around, I darted from one nook to the next, getting a few seconds of reprieve before I neared Danika's office. Very unfortunate that I had to pass it to reach the library. It was too late to double back when I realized the door was open a sliver and voices from behind it drifted to my ears. Obviously, I wasn't the only one thinking if I came in the early hours that no one would notice my presence here. And since I didn't value my life as much as I thought I did, my feet glided closer to the door, skirting around the empty desk before my brain caught up and realized what I was doing. My next breath got stuck in my throat when I recognized the person talking.

"... much as I'd like to agree with you, Mr. Blackman, I must do what is best for my coven. Surely you understand that." Danika's tone was coy, but it had just enough bite to tell whoever she was addressing that they were an idiot, as usual. What in all the hexes was she doing in her office this early?

"As I previously stated, you must see the exigency in the situation. You are Danika Byrne, for Hecate's sake. You don't have to do anything you don't want to. All I'm saying is we can manipulate the situation in a way that those fools will see only what we want them to see. I can't be the only one who knows the charade for what it is, right?" River had a note of desperation in his words, almost a pleading, which dumped a bucket of dread over my head.

I knew I should go because the conversation was not meant for my ears, but my peep-toes seemed glued to the floor, and my feet weighed a ton. Wiping my clammy hands on my clothing, I battled the dizziness threatening to take me to the floor, along with the heart palpitations rattling my ribcage.

"I cannot show favoritism, as you are well aware. What will that say for me as a leader? If the roles were reversed, I'm telling you now, I would not want to follow anyone who would seek personal gain over what was in the best interest of the coven." At that point, I reached the door, mushing my face as far as I could to peek through the tiny space. My grandmother stood behind her desk facing River, throwing her hands in the air as she spoke. "What do you expect me to do? Say no?"

"Yes." River widened his stance, and his arms folded stubbornly across his chest. "Yes, I do."

"I will most definitely not." Danika's chin jutted out, and she glared down her nose at him. The short hairs on my arms lifted with the static slapping me from her magic. "How dare you suggest for me to lie and manipulate!"

"She will be cast out, Danika. You can't be that fucking heartless." River growled, stepping up and slamming both hands on her desk with a loud smack. His voice rose with each word until he was practically shouting in her face.

"She is your blood. *Your* blood! You can't tell me you don't give a shit if she is dumped among the humans, because you and I both know they'll rip her apart. Need I remind you of all the witch hunts the humans have done throughout the centuries? How many we have lost, the many burned at the stake or drowned because we couldn't do shit. What do you think they'll do to her without the protection of the coven, huh? Welcome her with open arms?"

"Mind your tone, young man, or I will flay the skin off your bones." Danika's deceptively soft words made the floor under my feet rock back and forward, the soil under the building shivering in anticipation of the power blasting poor River to nothingness.

Any other day, I would've been gloating that she threatened him, but everything he said was playing on repeat in my head, and my blood had turned into shards of ice in my veins. Cast out? Witch hunts? Humans ripping me apart? Because there was no doubt in my mind that they were talking about me. One small part of the mass text message that brought me in the building in the first place stabbed my brain.

No exceptions.

It's not like I expected Danika Byrne to turn her back on what she thought was right for the coven, but hearing that she would chuck me to the wolves without thinking twice made traitorous tears prickle the back of my eyes. How was that for an eye opener? To have River fucking Blackman, the witch I thought was the enemy and the one I'd been hell bent on avoiding, care about my wellbeing more than my own flesh and blood? Tough love and all that shebang was all good and sound, but casting me out?

Somewhere in the back of my mind, I knew I'd

expected that from her, otherwise why would I be eavesdropping at that specific moment? It still smarted like a mofo to know it for sure, though. Numbing shock muddled my head for long enough that I missed whatever else River said. I'd give one thing to Blondie: he definitely didn't bend his spine under the weight of Danika's scowl, or her power. If anything, he seemed to grow when he stood, his spine snapping ramrod straight and his shoulders squaring.

"I will not sit back and watch." The growl was full of gravel, and if I didn't know he was a witch I would've sworn Danika was facing a shifter.

"You do what feels right to you, Mr. Blackman, and let us elders deal with what must be done." Dismissing him, she pulled her leather chair jerkily, lowering onto it.

If I would've moved a moment too soon and not been watching when River turned to leave her office with his head bent low to stare at his feet, I would've missed it. When his back was to her, my grandmother raised her head, and a small, secretive, and knowing smile tugged at her lips. My belly did acrobatics at the expression, at least until my predicament slapped me in the mug. Blondie was two steps from having a tete-a-tete with me, and I was just standing there like a shmuck.

My head whipped wildly as I jumped away from the slightly opened door, and in my panic, I dived for the empty desk at my side. Hecate must've heard my prayers because the chair was left pushed to the end, which allowed me to tuck myself under it. With my heart stuck to the roof of my mouth, I held my breath as the door was yanked fully open before slamming shut with enough force to rattle it on its hinges. River stomped past the desk, only to stop a few feet from it. My lungs screamed and burned from lack of oxygen. The idea of Blondie finding me on my hands and knees under the desk felt like an even worse outcome than being cast out by the only family I had left.

And what in all the hexes did Danika's smile mean?

Was she that happy to be rid of me?

Not that I could blame her, but still. It wasn't like I spent my time expecting everything to be served on a silver platter for me. I worked my ass off to train every single one of the losers in hand to hand, as well as weapon combat. I made it my mission to be the best at something since I couldn't help with magic. That counted for something, right?

Right?

I slapped a hand over my mouth when River walked away, and the breath I was holding whooshed out of me. My throat burned and my ribs hurt, but at least he didn't know I heard them. Forcing back the cough threatening to give me up, I scrambled to my feet, wanting to be as far away from Danika as I could. White noise thundered in my ears from the adrenaline, which was why I didn't hear anything around me. The moment I was on my feet, a hand pressed harshly over my mouth, and my body was yanked backward as whoever it was bodily carried me to the first office across the hall.

A scream lodged in my throat when they pushed me further into the empty office, and I stumbled a few steps before whirling around to face my attacker. Arms up and knees bent, I was ready to tackle the ass, maybe break an arm or a leg to teach them a lesson, when my glare locked on narrowed blue eyes I'd recognize in my sleep.

"What in the actual fuck, Sissily," I hissed at my best friend, my heartbeat drumming through my whole body as if it had a mind of its own. I was shaking like a leaf from the strength of it.

"You see that resting bitch face you have going over

there?" Her hip jutted to the side, and her finger swirled between us to encompass the air around my head. "*That* might work on everyone who doesn't know you, little jerk. I suggest next time, when you are planning to get rid of me just to get your dumb ass in trouble, you work harder on your expressions." Her thumb jabbed at the center of her chest. "*I* know you." Said thumb was replaced with a forefinger stabbing accusingly at my face. "You suck at lying."

While she was having a hissy fit and enjoying her monologue, I remembered River, and the top of my head started tingling.

"Did River see you?" My nails were biting at the skin of her shoulders before I was done talking, and I gave her a shake for good measure, too. "Did he?"

"I'm not dumb like you to crawl under desks. Of course he didn't see me." Sissily slapped my hands away, the dark smudges under her eyes while she glowered at me making the blue of her irises glow from within. With the ponytail still askew on the side of her head and her hair sticking out in all directions, she had the look of a crazed woman down pat. "Who spit in his coffee, by the way?"

"Huh?" My eloquent response was met with a roll of her peepers.

"Who. Pissed. Hottie. Off?" Every word was spoken slowly, her bow-shaped lips pronouncing them with exaggeration on each letter. Like a moron, I stared at her mouth until she was done, and her fingers snapped an inch from my nose. "Anyone home? Earth to Hazel."

I smacked her hand away.

"Don't be an ass." Hairs escaping her nutjob hairdo danced around her face when I blew a breath that came from my toes. "He had a disagreement with Danika." Acid scorched my gullet just thinking about it.

"About?" Brow arched, she stared at me so intently that it seemed like she was trying to read my mind to get the information faster.

Our voices were hushed, yet I still couldn't get the words out. Focused on the scar that sat above her left eyebrow in a straight line—courtesy of yours truly when she refused to give me my phone and of which she returned in kind, making us samesies now with matching disfigurements on our faces—I debated if we should drag her to the library or leave the building all together before Danika saw us and opened a fresh hell. I could always come back later and turn the library upside down until I found something to help me. Mind made up, I grabbed her hand and yanked her with me.

"I'll tell you when we are out of here." Her protests stopped at my muttered comment.

We snuck out of the empty office after I checked and double checked that no one was waiting to bust us out in the hall. Both of us darted on our tiptoes with single-minded determination, which, I might add, was easier for Sissily because, unlike my stupid ass with my stupid high heels, she had worn flats. No one yelled after us or stopped us to ask questions, and fresh air that didn't smell of herbs and melted wax slapped me in the face. With a sigh of relief, I dragged Sissily away from the coven and my grandmother's sight. Tears still burned the back of my eyes, and they had been there ever since I overheard the cursed conversation, but I refused to let them fall. Oh, no.

I had no intention of crying because she'd picked the coven over her own blood.

I wouldn't give anyone the satisfaction of doing that to me.

Anger replaced the soul-deep ache Danika had planted in my chest.

If my grandmother wanted to play games, I was going to give her a run for her money. She should've known better than to expect I'd sit around and just let this shit happen. I could be a player, too, and I had no doubt I'd win.

Lesson 5: *If you want to win at all costs, you play dirty.*

Chapter Eight

"There is no way she would do that," Sissily argued, adamantly trying to convince herself, while I held onto my steering wheel with a white-knuckled grip. We weren't moving, just sitting like idiots in my car because my best friend refused to use her own car and meet me somewhere away from ... well, just away. I didn't give two shits where.

"Right. Of course, she wouldn't. Don't be silly." My cheerful remark narrowed her gaze. "Danika knew someone would be eavesdropping. She staged the whole thing to teach me a lesson, and look at me now. I'm a new woman. Mission accomplished."

"We are focusing on the wrong thing." I had no idea how my neck didn't snap when I whipped my head to look at her. "River stood up for you. I told you he was not to be added in the same pile as Sasha Airborne."

She did say that. A time or two, or every second minute over the last couple of weeks, to be exact. If I didn't know Sissily better than I knew myself, I would've thought she had a crush on Blondie. Since we made a pact years ago that we both abided by, I knew that River could be prancing butt naked in front of her and Sissily would point him in my direction since I saw him first and we counted that as dibs. That was how we rolled. Our friendship meant more than a meatsuit with an attached penis to it. There were plenty of those around, but you only had one soul sister.

And she was my sister in every way that counted but blood.

"When was the last time you got laid? And, no. Impotent Mike does not count." I slashed the air between us when she opened her mouth. "Because River is not what we need to focus on, let me tell you. Maybe Davon was right from the beginning. I should've just registered as a human and got it over and done with. I didn't because I didn't want to embarrass Danika more than I already had just by existing as a dud, and look how she repaid me for it? She pushed me under a bus."

"First of all"—Sissily stuck her thumb up, starting a count, and I clenched my jaw because there was no stopping her when she started finger counting—"I have a dildo if I need an orgasm, which you know since that monstrosity was a gift from you when you thought you were being funny. Well, joke's on you, girlfriend. Second"—Her forefinger popped up— "River is very much something we should focus on because, unlike me with my dildo, you are the one who needs to get laid before your face freezes into a permanent scowl." Her middle finger jumped to join the other two. "Third, Davon the human has never been right about anything apart from how to do his job. If he was as smart as you want me to believe, he would've seen through all your acts for what they were. He failed the test because he couldn't get you to lower your walls, which means he wasn't worthy. That, my dear friend, makes him dumb."

"We are going off track—"

"Fourth"—Her ring finger popped up, and her glare deepened, shutting up my protests— "You will not pass now, or ever in the near or distant future, for a human, and I don't ever want you to say that again. Am I clear?"

My groan sounded pained, even to my own ears.

"Are. We. Clear. Hazel. Byrne?" She did that thing again where her lips looked twice the size they were while she pronounced every freaking letter in each word.

"I might not have a choice, girl." My shoulders slumped, and I deflated in the driver's seat like a balloon. "I hear what you're saying, but the reality does look bleak." My forefinger tapped the steering wheel like a nervous tic.

"What were you doing here anyway?" Sissily wiggled in the passenger seat to fully turn on her side and face me. Her jaw made a loud pop when she yawned wide and tucked one leg under her butt.

Hecate help me, I could kill my best friend from sleep deprivation.

"I was going to look for a spell, or … something." My shoulder twitched in a lazy attempt at a shrug while I stared ahead, unwilling to look at her. Saying it out loud made me realize how dumb of an idea it was, and my face warmed in shame. "You know a prepacked potion or already prepared spell won't work. They'll never accept it as proof of anything."

As usual, Sissily left me speechless, just like every other time as long as I'd known her, which was most of my life. If I expected pity or for her to feel sorry for me, I would be sorely mistaken. For the umpteenth time, I wished I could have as much faith in the impossible as she did, especially when it came to me.

"Hmmm, well a spell won't work, and you still need

magic to activate a potion, prepacked or freshly made. Incantation, however …" Lips pursed, her head wiggled side to side in thought. "If we find one for communing with a deity—which does not have to be Hecate because we DO NOT want to anger her, trust me—I strongly believe we can pull it off." Her unfocused gaze sharpened and locked on mine. But I could only gape at her. "What? How would they know what happened between you and one of the gods? You can totally bullshit your way through it, regaling them with tales of many blessings and guidance of trials ahead."

"You want me to lie to a board of the strongest witches in America?" It was difficult to hide the incredulity in my tone. I stared at her wide eyed like she'd grown three more heads.

"Yup." She released the "P" with a pop that made me flinch. "That's exactly what you are going to do, Hazel, or so Hecate help me, I will fry your ass right along with your entire wardrobe. Including all your shoes."

"You wouldn't," I gasped, but I knew that expression on her face and the manic glint in her eyes. She totally would, the little shit.

"Try me." It had to be the lack of sleep making her insane. It just had to be. Because Sissily looked like the product of a mad scientist on steroids, a mental patient having a baby—a feral one.

"Okay, okay, let's all calm down. There is no need for threats against my wardrobe. It has done nothing to you." Blowing out a deep breath, it took a few long moments to calm the galloping of my heart. I'd rather she had gone for my eyes than touch my clothing or, goddess forbid, my shoes. I still struggled with the gut-wrenching ache from destroying my designer ankle boots when I apprehended the Kashi demon.

"I knew you'd see reason and agree with me," Sissily cooed sweetly, honey dripping from her mouth.

"I didn't agree to shit." I jabbed my pointer finger in her face. "You bullied me into doing things your way."

"What can I say? I did learn from the best bully in the world. Bitch extraordinaire, Hazel Byrne." She yawned again, showing me her tonsils and molars before settling on a serene smile with eyelids half open. "Do you know her? She's amazing." My best friend chortled when I shook my head.

Unwanted as it was, the idea she planted in my head took root. My head was spinning with swirling thoughts. Could it be that easy? I was already thinking of an incantation, but I had no idea what kind to look for. Sissily made a good point with the call to a deity. Would I be able to pull it off? It wouldn't be the first time I bluffed my way out of things. Apart from Sasha Airborne, I actually hadn't hit anyone else. That bitch had deserved it, and I wasn't sorry. I had the scars to prove I had every right to break her nose and cheekbone. Okay, her arm too, but whatever. Everyone else after that ducked their heads or rushed to get away from me. Especially when I got in their faces with a bravado I'd perfected from insult after insult being thrown my way until even I believed I was ready to throw down and get dirty at any given moment. In reality though …

I didn't want to hurt or insult anyone.

All I wanted was to call them out on their bullshit.

The wielder of the truth stick, that was me.

"What I want to know, though, is why now?" It took me a moment to pull myself out of my head for her words to register. When I looked at her, she waved a hand between us as if dispersing the air. "Not what we are talking about. I mean, why are the other covens so adamant to do this shit now? Until this last meeting your grandmother attended, all of them were too happy to let us put our neck on the line with the scum of our world. We lost a lot of great witches to demon and rogue shifter bites, vampires and Fae gone feral. So, why now?"

"You can ask your buddy River ..." My scream made Sissily jerk in her seat when knuckles rapped on my window right next to my ear.

Fully focused on our conversation, neither one of us noticed anyone approaching my parked Mercedes. Panting, I struggled to inflate my lungs when I looked at the person leaning on top of my car with their forehead pillowed on their forearms. Like a deer in headlights, my gaze locked on River's, who was fighting to hold back a grin, his face twitching comically while his eyes danced with mirth on his handsome face.

"Speak of the devil and he shall find you," I muttered in frustration, jabbing the start button so I could lower the window. Sissily snickered next to me.

"Hi, River," my best friend chirped, ducking her head so she could see his face from the passenger seat. "What a pleasant surprise."

"Sissily." Blondie bestowed a panty-melting show of teeth at her as I debated whether or not I could yank him closer and close the window on his nose.

River Blackman had no right to be that perfect. Period.

"Don't listen to her, she's lying. It's been something she struggled with from a young age." I gave him a "what can you do" widening of my peepers. "How can I do you, Mr. Blackman." It took a herculean effort not to punch myself in the face for blurting that dumb shit out. "I mean ..." After an awkward clearing of my throat, I stared at the point in his chin so I didn't have to see his expression. "What do you want?" I barked.

Sissily snorted.

My face was on fire, and I hoped by some miracle Hecate found mercy on me and would strike me dead where I sat. River's body rocked slightly, and my heart lodged in my throat when I thought the goddess finally heard me and made the ground shake. That was when Sissily burst out laughing, almost busting my ear drum, and even going as far as doubling over and smacking her forehead on my upper arm. She wasn't laughing, actually; she was screaming with laughter. My owlish gaze snapped to Blondie, and that was apparently all he needed. Throwing his head back, River Blackman guffawed, the deep from the belly sounds rolling out of him in waves.

I dumbly stared at his tilted head and the strong column of his neck.

It wasn't Hecate granting my wish to kill me. That would've been merciful, indeed. River's body was rocking because he found my idiotic word vomit hilarious. Ugh. I had half a mind to sock Sissily if she didn't stop, too.

"You truly are the most intriguing person I have ever met, Miss Byrne," Blondie informed me with a wide smile, but only after he stopped chortling like a hyena. "You show this tough side of you to everyone but never the sweet, endearing one. I wonder why that is?"

"The deadliest poison is also the sweetest, Mr. Blackman." I batted my eyelashes at him before wiping all expressions from my face. "What do you want?"

His smile grew.

"Don't take it personal, River. She's always this awkward. Just give her some time," Sissily piped in, and I did sock her that time. "Ouch."

"Shut the hell up, you snake," I hissed at her, my glare promising glue instead of shampoo next time she washed her hair. She stuck her tongue out at me because that was how we showed maturity around these here parts.

"Duly noted, Miss Stormblood." River chuckled, shaking his head at me.

It was always strange when someone addressed Sissily by her family name. I had no idea why. Maybe because we were inseparable, and it was a shock to hear it was different from mine. Or she was friendly with everyone and they always felt comfortable using her first name, unlike me. I was the cactus to her tulip. She allowed everyone in her personal bubble to bask in her beauty and warmth, while I was only too happy to stab them with my thorns. Well, stab anyone but her, unless she didn't stop laughing at me. If she didn't, I could stab her in the forehead since she was close enough.

"Whatever you are thinking, no." My best friend scooted far away from me, slicing the air between us. "Just no."

"I'm sorry to interrupt, ladies," River started.

"Are you?" I growled at him in annoyance. "Sorry enough to go away? No? Shame, that."

"We have a teeny tiny problem." There was no humor left, which cast his features in dangerous territory for my stupid hormones.

"You should know all about teeny tiny, I guess." I suppressed a groan when Sissily pinched me hard for muttering under my nose.

"What's up?" she asked River, ignoring the death looks I was stabbing at the side of her face.

River looked left and right as if making sure no one was around before crouching, stopping only when he was eye level with us across the window. My heart skipped a beat having his face that close, especially when I noticed the golden flakes in his melted chocolate irises. They blinked like stars as the sun hit them through his thick, long lashes.

"I'm sure you both received the message this morning." He didn't need to explain which message, and we didn't ask. "It's in Hazel's best interest for this to stay between us, but …" His gaze flicked through mine, and his jaw tightened. "I think this is not just other covens feeling left out when it comes to enforcing the law."

"Oh?" Sissily sounded way too nonchalant.

I, on the other hand, found it hard to breathe.

"This is all my observation, of course, but I have a suspicion someone is trying to get rid of the Byrne bloodline. Starting with Hazel."

"Aren't you under 'other covens' too?" I couldn't stop the words when they slipped from my lips without a conscious thought.

"I am, yes." His peepers swirled with power when he focused on me, and there was not enough air to fill my lungs even with the window of the car open. "But as I told you a few times, I find you very intriguing. A puzzle I would love to solve. I would like to keep you around, if you don't mind."

His nearness made me dizzy all on its own, the scent of his cologne causing feathers to tickle the back of my throat and my belly to tighten. Adding a plot to remove me from my coven and a threat to my family, regardless of all the faults we had, poured acid in the pit of my stomach. Bile burned my windpipe, and my throat worked double-time to swallow it down.

"What do you suggest?" Sissily was all business while I struggled not to pass out.

"Not here." River stood up, tapping the roof of my car once. "Meet me at Moon Howl café. First one there orders coffee."

We watched him swagger away like he didn't just drop the mother of all bombs on my head with no warning. Sissily was quiet as she stared through the windshield, and I replayed the conversation I'd overheard between Danika and River. With that in mind, what Blondie said made sense. His words, the ones he didn't know I'd heard, aligned with his declaration that he wanted to help. I closed the window and yanked on my seatbelt, clicking it in place. Sissily did the same.

"Let's hope he knows CPR because one of us might end up with a heart attack after one more coffee." Sissily snorted, but there was barely any humor in it. She was lost in thought. I zoomed out of the parking lot like a bat out of hell, wondering how Blondie knew to pick our favorite café to meet up. The intuition that couldn't be an intuition since I was without magic tickled the back of my mind. He didn't make a comment about my best friend's disheveled look either, like seeing the always-put-together Sissily resembling a mad woman was an everyday thing. So, it came down to a couple of things warring for attention in my head.

I trusted that there was some sort of ploy in the works with the full moon ritual.

And I just didn't know if I could trust River Blackman.

Chapter Nine

Getting to the café was a true miracle with my head full of buzzing thoughts. Sissily had to shout a few times at me to watch it, and I was pretty sure her foot made a hole in my car because she was slamming it on a nonexistent brake. Not that I wanted to be a jerk or anything, I just had to get to our destination as fast as I could and hear what River thought was too dangerous to say around the coven building. Whatever it was, it didn't bode well for me.

I was one hundred percent certain of that.

"We can't do shit if we are pancakes under a damn truck," Sissily grated through her teeth, clinging to the sidebar for dear life.

"Oh, ye of little faith." She literally hissed at me like a feral cat when I muttered those words, and her hiss only grew louder when I zigzagged through traffic.

"Hazel, I will murder you in your sleep if you don't slow down."

"You'll need to bypass Danika to do that, so yeah, not scared." The heel of my palm smacked the horn at the old lady in the Buick clinging to her steering wheel as if she was trying to hump it. "Get off the road if you can't drive, old bat."

"Maybe you can work on your road rage." Swallowing audibly, my best friend was developing a green tinge to her skin when I gave her a side-eyed glance.

We were nearly there, so I eased off the gas. I couldn't help but snort when Sissily slumped in her seat, the relief pulsating from her. It wasn't the first time she complained about me driving too fast. It was a regular occurrence, which was why we drove separately most of the time and met wherever we were going.

"It's true magic how you haven't caused an accident when you are behind the wheel."

"You think it might work as a contribution on Saturday?" When she cocked her head to gape at me, I snickered. "What? You said it was magic."

Her shaking hand snapped to point a finger across the street at the door of the Moon Howl. "River is here."

"And you bitch about me driving fast?" Irked that Blondie beat me there, I took a sharp turn toward the open parking opposite the café.

Okay, I was more peeved that he looked like some golden god posing for a Hell brochure, with his hands in his pockets and aviators perched on his nose. The only thing missing was a sign above his head saying "*Sinners welcome,*" and for me to snap a shot. Lucifer would have a line all the way to the pearly gates full of women waiting to get in.

What was it about River that made me act like a thirteen-year-old having a tantrum?

My tires screeched when I squeezed the Mercedes between two SUV's, and Sissily practically threw herself out of my car. While she clutched the door until her legs stopped shaking, I yanked my purse closer and dug for my phone. It was on silent when I thought I was going to the library, so after putting the ringer back on, I jumped out too. Giving her a break, I offered her my hand, and she took it gratefully, crushing my fingers in the process.

"You are so dramatic." It took a couple of tugs to free my poor fingers, and I tucked her hand at my elbow.

Stressed or not, I had to smile when she muttered all sorts of unflattering things under her breath, her crooked ponytail bobbing on the side of her head. I didn't look any better either, but my hair didn't resemble a nest at least. Which I pointed out to her, by the way, before my heart did a punch-shrivel-punch the second my eyes locked on River. Blondie was watching us from across the street over his aviators as if he knew exactly which exit we'd use, causing my belly to dip dangerously. It was obvious that he knew my reaction to him judging by the curl of his mouth and the twinkle in his peepers.

"Drinks are on me," he said as a way of greeting when we reached him, and I stared dumbly at his back when he pivoted to enter the café.

Sissily dragged my ass to catch up to him.

I, on the other hand, narrowed my eyes on River, watching every twitch and sway his body made as he moved deeper inside the large room. There was something in the roll of his shoulders, or maybe it was the way his feet glided instead of pressing on the ground when he walked, as if they did the earth a favor by walking on it, that rubbed me wrong. If it wasn't the middle of the day and if I didn't know he was a witch, I would've pegged him for a vampire simply by the way he walked. He possessed the magnetic allure of the vamps like it was his goddess given right, as well as the predatory prowl no mere witch could perfect. Not to that degree, in any case.

It was setting alarms off in my monkey brain that were telling me to run and not look back.

Which was dumb on so many levels. Because I had no doubt I could knock River Blackman on his ass blindfolded. So, what was it that warned me about him?

"No need to be that prickly, Miss Byrne." Blondie grinned at me over his shoulder. "I mean no harm. I swear it."

The chair scraped loudly across the floor when I yanked it out to take a seat, and he chuckled, while Sissily would've made a teen die of envy with her eye roll. My whole life was tipping sideways, and they cared about stupidities like me playing a hedgehog or not. Hecate help me, I was ready to lose my shit and start screaming like a loon.

"You are not that special, Blackman, I'm like that with everyone." Twisting to wrap my purse over the back of the chair, I didn't miss the twitch of his mouth.

"She's not lying," Sissily chirped, all too happy to be on firm ground instead of in my car. "That's how she shows her charm, by glaring at everyone."

"Ha, ha. I'm sitting right here, so let's not talk about me in third person, mmm-kay? Can we get to the point?" It was a hard task not to fidget under River's intense gaze, but I managed.

Sissily raised a finger when the barista called her name, our coffees ready before we even thought about ordering. "River, what do you want?" she asked him, her ass halfway off her seat already.

"Double espresso, please. Black." My forehead pinched when he ordered the same thing as me while he shoved dollar bills in Sissily's hand. "I said I'm buying." He waved her off when she protested.

"Everyone apart from the human police officer," he said to me in a low tone when Sissily rushed to grab our drinks.

"What?" If my eyebrows went any lower, I could've used them as eyelids.

"You were not prickly with the cop." The melted chocolate of his irises darkened, and I involuntarily gulped, which pissed me off. "As a matter of fact, I remember you being very touchy-feely with the human."

"My personal life does not concern you, River." I bet Amber and Alex would've been proud if they heard my growl. "Stay out of it."

"You see, Hazel," he drawled as if to point out the fact that I'd skipped the formalities first by using his name. I seethed in my chair. "The way I see it, at this point, everything concerns me when it comes to you."

"Like hell—"

"I couldn't care less what you do and who you do it with as long as we keep things as they are past Saturday." He spoke over me just as Sissily returned, placing our coffees on the table. I expected him to stop with her there, but as always, he surprised me. "Until then, I don't trust anyone around you."

Sissily cocked an eyebrow.

"Apart from you, obviously," Blondie amended.

Amber was throwing cautious glances our way, so I forced a smile, giving her a thumbs-up to let her know we were good. That lady was one in a million being able to run a business, chat with her regulars, and still keep an eye on us. There was no doubt if she thought something was wrong, her mate would be looming over our table in less than five minutes. It was a mystery how the Alpha managed to do things but never be far from his mate.

"Let's hear it, River. I'm tired, hungry, and starting to get bored. What's this conspiracy you mentioned." After everything that happened—and it wasn't dinner time yet—my patience was nonexistent.

"There's been talk about covens taking too much power, and it's time for other factions to take over the enforcing of the law," he started barely above a whisper, making me lean toward him to hear better.

"I bet the vamps will love that, won't they," Sissily hissed, while I grimaced when I chugged the coffee and blistered the roof of my mouth. "Do you need a bib?" she snapped.

"No, but you might if I punch you in the nose." My fingers wiggled in the glass of water she wisely provided to fish out an ice cube. I thought my tongue was burned too, not just the roof of my mouth. "How come we knew nothing about it? That sounds like some shit Danika would be all over," I mumbled around the ice in my mouth.

It felt like the cube got stuck in my throat when I saw the pitying look on River's face, but it didn't take him long to school his features into a blank mask. Sissily reached for my hand, giving it a reassuring squeeze, and those treacherous tears pricked the back of my eyes. Right, Danika didn't share important things with a dud. How silly of me to assume otherwise. For some reason, I found myself staring at the cufflinks around River's wrists where he had his forearms pressed on the table.

I guess it wasn't just me playing the "dress to impress" card.

And I was deflecting.

"What do I have to do with any of it?" The ice shattered with a loud crunch in my mouth when I chomped on it angrily. "I'll cheer whoever it is on if they stop those assholes from hunting rogues and ferals. If I'm not allowed to do it, they shouldn't be either. Someone else takes over, my coven can't hold my lack of magic over my head. Where do I sign?"

"It's not that simple." River cocked his head, eyeing me like I'd grown horns or a second head. "The shifters want nothing to do with it unless it involves their packs. The Fae are so paranoid about protecting their magic that it'll be anarchy before you know it, which leaves the demons and the vampires. If the demons take over, we will regret the days we were born. If the vampires take the mantle, it'll be us doing all the hard work again with nothing to show for it. It's a no-win situation, so might as well keep everything the way it is."

"Why are you telling me all this?" My arms crossed defensively over my chest, squishing my boobs. Sissily had a thoughtful look on her face I really didn't like. "I want nothing to do with the politics of our world, and I never have." But I knew what was up. He didn't need to spell it out for me.

They wanted Danika out of the picture, and I was their way in.

"Let's not pretend that my grandmother will sit back and let them do whatever to protect me. Danika will die before allowing anyone to blackmail her or take her coven. You should feel sorry for those who try, not be worried about me." Feeling the urge to point out the pink elephant in the room, I huffed in annoyance. "She will never choose me over the coven. You know it, I know it, and everyone else knows it. If their plan is to hit her through me, I actually feel sorry for the idiots."

Sissily said nothing to that because I spoke the truth.

"I think you are wrong," River argued, but he didn't sound like he believed it himself.

I debated if I should tell him that I heard half of the conversation he had with my grandmother but decided against it. Something nagged at me to keep my mouth shut, and for now, I would listen.

"We can still prepare for Saturday the way we planned." Sissily speared me with a pointed look, though she didn't go into details about our crazy plan in front of Blondie. "If that doesn't work, we will play it by ear. We work best under pressure, anyway." Her shrug was twitchy, betraying her unease.

"We"—My finger flicked between us— "are not playing, period. If it doesn't work, you are getting your ass out of there and pretending you don't know me from Adam. Understand?"

"Can I hear of this plan?" Blackman asked in a hesitant drawl.

"No," Sissily and I said at the same time.

"I can't help if I don't know what's going on." His hands rose to the sides in surrender, and he leaned away from us.

"I appreciate you sharing what you suspect is going on with us, River." Biting back my annoyance, which was wrongly aimed at him, I sagged with a sigh. "I really do. But it's best for everyone at this table to stay away from me on Saturday. Whatever happens, I don't want anyone getting in trouble or, goddess help me, getting hurt because of me. I can deal with whatever Danika decides to do. I'm used to it."

My best friend was grinding her teeth so hard I could hear her molars scraping, but I couldn't get a read on

Blondie. There was an expression on his face I couldn't truly grasp, or more like I refused to. Maybe he had some misplaced hero complex and that was the reason for all this info sharing. Everything else was too messed up to take into consideration. Which gave me an idea.

"I would, however, ask you for a favor. If you don't mind." My gaze stayed level on River, or I would've missed the barely noticeable straightening of his shoulders.

"Name it, and if it's in my power, consider it done." He played right into it as I'd hoped.

"When it's time for me to face the Council, I need you to take Sissily out of there."

"Like hell you'll push me away when you need me most," Sissily snarled, her teeth bared at me. "Fuck you, Hazel, if you think I'll hide while they decide your fate."

River was watching me silently, his eyes darting over my face.

I waited.

"I don't need your permission to do anything, by the way." Sissily was getting angrier with each word, and venom coated every word she spoke. "And you, River." She rounded on him, but he didn't look away from me. "I will fry your ass to kingdom come if you get anywhere near me on Saturday. Hecate help me, I'll kill you if it's the last thing I do, you hear me?"

"Deal," River said to me.

All our phones chimed at the same time, cutting off the rest of the death threats my best friend had planned to throw at Blackman. Sending a thank you to Hecate, I fished my iPhone from my purse, and adrenaline spiked in my veins when I opened the message. A rogue demon was holding humans hostage in their home. And as luck would have it, the address was not even five minutes away from the café.

What were the odds twice in two weeks for me to be the closest witch to answer the call? River and Sissily not included, of course.

"Chug-a-lug, peeps. We have a demon to kill." Gulping my espresso in one swallow, I jumped up, slugging the purse over my shoulder.

I power walked to my car after I waved at Amber, worried they'd stop me from going after the rogue. Surprisingly, neither River nor Sissily said a word about me going on the hunt. My best friend was still busy enlightening River about all the ways she knew how to melt his organs if he touched her on Saturday. Blondie was too busy staring at me like I was one of the greatest mysteries of the known world.

Me?

Jittery and high on caffeine, I was shaking in my peep-toes from excitement. All the anger from hearing Danika say she didn't give two shits about what would happen to me would have an outlet.

I was skipping on the way to the car as I imagined all the ways I was going to beat the crap out of the demon.

Chapter Ten

Okay, so I couldn't really beat the shit out of the demon.

That became obvious the moment I reached the apartment door after rushing up the stairs two at a time to the fourth floor. First, the said door was leaning sideways like a drunk sailor holding onto the frame by the top hinge. Smears of something black were smudged on both sides of the hallway, and a rancid stench potent enough to peel paint off drywall wafted from the apartment. Sulfur and the heavy odor from black demon magic made the air so thick and heavy it was almost tangible.

Second, the demon had a buddy who blocked the doorway and was staring me down with red, glowing peepers. Even without the whole dramatic flair from the red eyes, it was easy to recognize what type of demon I was dealing with. The beautiful woman in front of me that belonged on the cover of a magazine rather than blocking a doorway, with murder written on her pretty face, could've passed for human if she wasn't being a drama llama, but the backward hands were a dead giveaway to a witch like me. Her silky red dress clung to her body like a second skin, pushing her boobs to her chin, and her platinum hair cascaded over her shoulders like liquid silver while she pursed her lips and eyed me up and down, finding me lacking most probably.

Rakshasa demons had those backward hands to help them in hand-to-hand combat because the attacks usually came from unusual and unexpected angles, confusing their opponent until they ripped them to shreds or siphoned their soul. They also changed into animals or nightmarish monsters in a very different way from shifters. Rakshasa needed a ready body to jump into—no matter if she found it lacking or not—if they wanted to change, hence the soul sucking thing they had going on. That gave me my main priority.

I had to make sure my body was not used as a meat suit.

Blindly running into a situation was never a smart idea—there was a lesson there somewhere I was sure—but I wanted to reach the place before River and Sissily. The two witches in question were thumping up the stairs already, and I had too much suppressed anger to wait until they caught up with me. Backward hands or not, I was prepared to face a Rakshasa demon. Maybe not two of them, but one for sure. I even had a practice dummy in my basement, which I dismembered by placing the hands backward so I could train myself for this specific situation.

"It's rude not to invite me in when I rushed to get here," I told the demon, and the bitch smiled, a toothy grin displaying two overlapping rows of sharp teeth like a damn shark under her pouty red lips. "And I'll need the number of your dentist. It's hard to reach that perfection of white these days."

"Why don't you come closer, witch?" My palm itched to slap myself for waving my hand at her because she saw the pentagram tattoo on my forefinger.

My saving grace was the fact that I stayed away from gatherings, so only a handful could recognize me as the infamous dud of Gatekeeper's Coven. Flashing my tattoo, though, presented a big problem for me. The demon would expect magic, and would fight with it, too. Fuck a duck on a stick.

"I have manners." River and Sissily were on the first floor already. "I don't barge in uninvited." Keeping her eyes on my face, I slid an inch closer.

"Come on in, then." Her arms folded at the small of her back, hiding them from my view as she stepped to the side.

A whimper came from somewhere in the apartment, but it was cut short. My stomach dropped to my feet. I knew there were two Rakshasas because their disgusting demonic powers were crawling all over my skin. Not for the first time, I wondered if humans felt the "other" since they were magicless like me, the sensation like an army of fire ants using my body as a sugar cube to munch on.

Poised to attack the moment I was close enough, I moved toward the demon. At the last minute, I decided to change tactics, and as soon as I was halfway across the hallway, I pounced. I swung my purse wide, socking the Rakshasa in the head when I released the handles. Both her arms came up to protect her face, but I was on her already, my fists hammering at any opening I had. Bones crunched under my knuckles when we went down in a heap of limbs a couple of feet past the broken door. Breath sawing in and out through clenched teeth, I made the mistake of glancing inside the apartment to check for the location of the second demon.

And I lost the advantage of the surprise attack.

My head turned into a tunnel with a shrieking train passing through when she caught me at the temple with a backhanded fist. The hit doubled my vision, giving her two heads and two mouths filled with those teeth. Black blood dripped from her nose and split lip, yet she was grinning like a piranha when she yanked my head back by a fistful of hair.

Lesson 6: *Long hair, unless wrapped in a tight bun, will fuck you over in a fight.*

There was nothing in this life I hated more than someone grabbing my hair.

It made me black out.

Rage bubbled until my skin was warm with it, and I jerked out of her grip with a snarl, leaving ripped strands hanging limply from her fingers. My scalp was on fire and hot liquid drenched my head, plastering my hair to it. My blood was flowing freely down my scalp. I fell back, catching my weight on my hands just in time to kick out with all the strength I could muster. It was satisfying to hear her shriek when the heel of my peep-toes sunk into her side. Pulling my leg back, I did it again and again, each time punching a new hole in her upper body.

Then the magic came.

Burgundy tendrils snaked out from the Rakshasa's hands, hissing and snapping at me like living snakes. Blisters filled with a sickly beige fluid popped out everywhere it made contact with my skin. The damn magic was eating through muscle while I screamed, and it was coming from two sides instead of just the demon I was fighting. The second demon decided to help his buddy, and I wished it hadn't. Not because I was burning alive. Because that one was the scariest thing I'd ever seen in my life, and that announced him as the male in the duo. Terror tried to lock me in its grip, but a cry coming from whoever they held hostage in the apartment snapped me out of it.

Unlike the rest of my kind, I actually took it personally when humans were attacked. That was the main reason I stuck my nose where it didn't belong—much to Danika's dismay—but I couldn't help myself. They were just like me, only I was stronger and would live much longer. Because they were magicless, every asshole thought they were free for the picking.

I strongly disagreed.

The pained cry not only snapped me out of the terror but gave me the strength I needed. Desperate to reach them so I could protect them better, I wildly swung with my fists and kicked out with both legs. The Rakshasa didn't expect me to move with the magic her buddy was waving, so I stabbed my heel in her eye, the thin point cracking her skull and poking through the bone. It stuck out at the top of her head like a newly grown horn. I had to kick off the other shoe so I didn't limp around like a fool, and all because of a demon for the second time. Another pair of shoes ruined by damn demons. Soon, I had every intention to mail an invoice directly to Hell for my damages.

My foot pulled out, leaving my poor peep-toe hanging in front of the female Rakshasa's face, and I scrambled up to face the male. At eight feet, he hunched low so his head didn't go through the ceiling of the apartment. The demon's body was some butchered version of a Frankenstein monster, if said fictional creature had made his body out of different animal parts. Fur stuck out in tufts from some parts, while others were covered in scales or wrinkled hides. Two tails twitched around the area of his ass in agitation. Instead of a mouth, there was a beak, the tip sharp enough to go through steel, and three sets of backward arms were spread wide as if ready to snatch me if I dared get close enough.

I had every intention to get close enough.

Jaw clenched and seething in anger because my skin was still trying to eat itself from their damn magic, I screamed from the top of my lungs like a banshee and charged him raging-bull style. It must've been a first for the demon to fight an idiot like me because he stood like a lump when my head connected with his sternum. There was a crack in my neck, and a sharp pain zapped from the base of my skull through my shoulders when we collided, but much to my surprise, we both went down. Furniture and other decorative objects broke when the demon's body plowed through them, and I landed sprawled over his chest. My left hand gripped around the floor blindly in search of anything I could use to kill him, and this was all while I avoided his beak because he was shaking his head at me the whole time.

My fingers wrapped around something long—a lamp base maybe—and I raised it above my head to stab it in his throat. My nose burned from the stench of sulfur coming off him, and water pooled in my eyes, blurring my vision. Just before the object sank into his head, the demon's eyes regained their focus, and he swatted me off him like a fly. I rolled before coming up in a crouch just as I heard my coven mates at the front door.

"Hazel," Sissily yelled, the panic in her voice stabbing me in the heart. "HAZEL!"

"In here," I called out, backing up until my butt found a wall so I could scan the space.

Wide, innocent eyes the color of clear skies locked on me from behind an armchair that was pushed in a corner. I nearly doubled over seeing the young boy trembling in fear and clutching his younger brother while tears rolled down their faces. Dried blood was caked in their hair, and there was enough of it that I could hardly tell what color it would be when it was clean. The boy's hand was shaking so hard he nearly hit his brother in the face when he raised it to press a finger to his lips, asking me to not give them away. The chair was angled in the corner of the room, so the poor children must've thought they could hide and not be found behind it.

Their father was a bloody mess swaying on his feet in front of the armchair, though he was still determined to protect them from the monster invading their home. His wife's dead body was at his feet, her blue eyes the same color as her son's staring at me unseeing.

Something inside me broke.

River materialized at the entrance of the ripped-apart living room, fury twisting his otherwise handsome face. His eyes darted from me and my blistered skin to the barely standing man and dead woman. My lungs were burning from the need to fill them with oxygen, but I wasn't able. When I spoke, it felt like someone was pulling barbed wire through my throat, and my voice was unrecognizable.

"Protect the children."

Blackman's eyes widened for a split second.

He didn't give me a chance to move.

In a split second, he transformed into a creature with a

body made of flames, and lightning spit from his fingers. The stale air in the apartment filled with the scent of ozone, which covered the stench of blood and sweat I smelled when I entered. The male demon was still struggling to stand when River was on him, the impact blinding me when the fire burst around both of them like a cloud. Numb from shock, I stood stunned because it didn't burn anything but the demon. No, everything else seemed to have a barrier, protecting it from River's magic.

The roar of a wounded animal shook the walls of the building.

My head whipped to the empty doorway of the living room when something small darted inside, but the only thing I saw was Sissily dashing right for the swaying man, who was watching everything with too-wide eyes and a blanched-of-color face. It was enough to propel me into action too, and I dove for the two boys curled up in the corner. The man started screaming at my friend when she attempted to get him out of the room, but I had no time to assure him that his children would follow.

The older boy scratched at my arms when I tugged his younger brother out of his grasp, only to proceed climbing me like a monkey when he realized I was trying to get them out of there. "Hold tight," I croaked, unable to speak from the death grip the child had on my windpipe. Both children had their faces buried, one in the crook of my neck and the other my chest as I made a mad dash for the hallway, almost tripping over a broken table. Sissily was on my heels with the father, now dragging him behind her.

I knew he would follow when he saw his boys.

"Stay here, Hazel. I'll go help River." My friend panted, and disappeared inside the apartment the moment we had the humans out of immediate danger.

While trying to get the boys out, I'd forgotten all about my blistered skin until mind-numbing pain reminded me of it. Everywhere the children clung to me felt like fresh hell opening its embrace to pull me under. My whimper was pathetic when the father took hold of his young, hugging them to his chest as if I might steal them from him. Crashing and screams echoed from the apartment, River and Sissily's voices barely audible through the shrieks.

"My wife," the man rasped, and my heart broke all over again when fat tears ran down the mess of his face.

His left cheek was slashed open, the swelling enough to close his one eye. Blood dripped from his temple, and he was shaking hard enough to rattle his children. Both boys were crying softly, each sound stabbing me deeper and deeper in my soul. With my back pressed against the wall in the hallway, I slid next to where the human was kneeling, not daring to lose eye contact. I hated everything I was, everything we were as "other" when I saw the desperation in his gaze begging me to tell him she was alive, that my coven mates would save her too.

"I'm sorry." My choked-out whisper wasn't something he should've heard, yet he did. "I'm so, so sorry." His image blurred.

I honored him by not looking away when heart-wrenching sobs rocked his body and he curled over his children. I kept whispering apologies while my own dam opened, unchecked tears rushing down my face in a torrent. My shaking hand reached for the older boy when I noticed him watching me with an expression in his eyes I couldn't name, though it sent a shiver down my spine. His tiny fingers snatched my trembling ones, and all sound stopped like someone had pressed pause.

River filled the doorway of the apartment, his hair tousled and his eyes wild.

"Sissily, take care of the humans," he barked over his shoulder before he advanced on me with the determination of a desperate man.

The last thing I remembered was the boy screaming at River not to take me away.

Then everything went dark.

Chapter Eleven

When I'd rushed to get my ass kicked by Rakshasa demons, I didn't expect to find myself in the coven's infirmary with Danika glaring down her nose at me. Or with River holding my hand like a drowning man would hold a straw, but that was neither here nor there. I had bigger problems to deal with judging by the anger on my grandmother's face and my body being wrapped up mummy style from neck to hip. To buy myself some time, I jutted my chin and pointed at the glass of cold water sitting next to my bed that was dripping condensation on the side table. My mouth chose that moment to remind me that it felt like the Sahara, and I nearly choked when I tried to swallow.

My best friend, who I didn't notice at first, hip-bumped River to get him out of the way so she could stick the straw between my lips. Hoping Sissily could see the gratitude in my unfocused eyes, I sucked on the water so hard some of it dribbled from the corners of my lips. It caused one hell of a coughing fit, but at least my tongue wasn't stuck to the roof of my mouth.

"Easy, girl," Sissily chided, the worry in her gaze sending tendrils of trepidation through me.

Danika, on the other hand, had no qualms about speaking her mind now that I was apparently awake. "What I would like to know is this: what were the three of you doing there in the first place?" She glowered at me for most of that but turned those piercing eyes on River at the last second.

Good, let Blondie deal with her to see how it felt.

"When the message came, we were having coffee at Moon Howl, and we were the closest witches in the vicinity." If he wasn't crushing my fingers, I never would've guessed how pissed River was by the calm tone of his voice.

"Hazel shouldn't be anywhere near a rogue or a feral, Mr. Blackman. You should know better than that." My grandmother could cut metal with her sharp words. "And you, Sissily, what were you thinking?" She rounded on my best friend.

"Okay, you know what?" I piped in when Sissily opened her mouth, no doubt to defend herself and me. "How about everyone stop talking about me like I'm not just sitting here like a lump, mm-kay? It's pretty bad when I need to repeat myself with that ten times a day. You see where I'm going with this?"

Danika seethed.

"No? Let me clear it up so you can move forward." River tried to keep hold of my hand, but I yanked it out, groaning and huffing until I was half-sitting and half-leaning on the narrow bed. It pissed me off when I felt my bare ass gliding over the thin sheet where the hospital gown parted with my movement.

"Hazel"—Gaze locked on Danika, I had to force the words through my teeth— "is capable of making her own decisions, thank you very much. You can thank yourself for my stubborn ass since I'm a product of your parental guidance. As for the clusterfuck we walked into, how about instead of reading me my rights like some pompous ass, you tell me what in the actual fuck is going on?" Everything came out in a rush.

"Don't be crude, Hazel Byrne." Danika huffed at me in annoyance, but her lips did twitch when I mentioned the tough-love methods she'd used to raise me.

And she was deflecting.

Go figure.

"This is the second time in two weeks there was a demon doing dumb shit, so let's focus on that, mm-kay." While River had his plump lips pressed tight enough to form a white line on his face, Sissily was trying to blend in with her surroundings just to stay out of it. "Instead of worrying about me, I think you need to talk to whoever is in charge of them right now and ask why they are running around killing humans and selling illegal body parts."

"Don't tell me how to do my job," my grandmother snapped, done with my mouthing off. Tough luck for her. I already knew what her next words would be, so I was ready for them. "One of these days, you'll get it through your thick head that you have no magic. Either that will come first, or I'll be left to bury you instead of the other way around, you stupid girl."

I wasn't sure what surprised me more. The fact that, for the first time, her words didn't open the unhealed wound in my heart and make it bleed all over my insides and pride, or the animalistic growl coming from deep in River's chest that raised the short hairs on the back of my neck. Even Danika took a step back from him, eyeing him like he was a snake ready to bite.

"I need to speak to my granddaughter alone."

"I don't think so." River jumped to his feet from the metal chair to face her, folding his arms across his chest. "We were all there, so we all need to hear whatever it is you want to say, with all due respect. Also, Hazel made a very valid point. It will take me a month to find a record of one, little less two Rakshasa demons attacking in the middle of the day."

"Spill," I added my two cents when he was done.

After a very long, very uncomfortable moment of Danika looking each of us up and down, she did something so uncharacteristic of her that I fully expected Earth to be smacked with a meteor and for all of us to die. With a heavy sigh, she cracked her neck, first left and then right, before she turned her eyes up to stare at the ceiling like she was asking Hecate to help her. My heart galloped in my chest, and my fingers tingled while I watched her debate how much to tell us.

Danika was a mountain. There was nothing shy of a natural disaster that could shake the woman, and seeing her tiredly move to my bed to perch on it like her legs could barely hold her left me holding my breath. As much as I was dying to know what was going on, I also wished I'd never breached the subject. Humans loved saying ignorance is bliss, but in our world, that took it to a whole new level. If it didn't involve me, and the little boy's frightened eyes didn't haunt me by being burned into my memory, I would've asked her to keep whatever it was to herself. The images of the man curled around his children while he cried kept my mouth glued shut and my spine straight.

"There have been some changes in the hierarchy of a couple of the factions in the last six months or so." My grandmother tucked a loose strand of silky hair behind her ear, folding one leg under her to get comfier. Absently, her hand smoothed nonexistent wrinkles on her black floor-length dress, and she watched the movement with rapt attention. "It disturbed the order we've fought hard to maintain, as well as caused discord among the ranks for the rest of us."

My gaze found Sissily's to check if my friend was thinking the same thing. That meeting that caused all my problems where I could be cast out in about twenty-four hours, not just from my coven but my world, must've been called because of what Danika was telling us. We both had an "oh shit" moment, unlike River, who was standing frozen like a guard next to my bed. It was obvious he knew some of it.

"So, some demons are acting up like unsupervised children while they select a new leader?" I meant to play down the gravity of the situation, but my voice came off weak and turned my statement into a question.

Danika hummed noncommittally. "You could say that …"

"Did they choose to start a war with witches while they were running loose?" Sissily spoke the words I was already thinking, reading them from my expression most probably.

"It sure sounds like it if they decided to concentrate their attacks in Cleveland of all places." My grandmother's sharp look in my direction almost made me laugh. Did she think I was stupid just because I had no magic? "Out of all the places in the world, they picked the city where the Gatekeeper's Coven is stationed full of magic using enforcers. Almost as if they have a personal grudge against us."

My heart stuttered for a moment before it kicked into overdrive when Danika's face blanched of all color. Frantically, I replayed what I said in my head but couldn't find one thing that would scare Danika Byrne. The air in the small room felt too thin, making my lungs burn from lack of oxygen. Then River added one more nail in the proverbial coffin when he opened his mouth.

"The demon discord is the reason for the presentations on Saturday night, isn't it?"

"In a way." It seemed like that was all Danika could say because I knew she didn't want to tell us the truth. It was written all over her pale face.

Then she surprised me more than any other time in my life.

"Mr. Blackman, be a dear and activate a silence circle if you don't mind." With a sigh, she pressed the bridge of her nose.

I was hyperventilating at that point. What in the monkey's hairy balls was going on to make Danika scared she might get overheard? Not once had I seen her think twice to bark out the first thing that came to her mind, not giving two shits if she hurt someone's feelings in the process. That was the reason I stayed silent with my eyes glued to her face, while River muttered under his breath, flicking his fingers occasionally as he stopped at all four corners of the room. Goosebumps popped up on my arms when he was done, the bubble of magic forming around us. I would've envied the ease with which he did that if I wasn't freaking out internally. My tattoo tingled in reaction to his power, impotent as it might be. My tattoo, not River's magic.

"As you all know, for the demons to have a new leader, the old one must die." Well, no, not all of us knew that, fuck you very much, but I wanted to hear the rest so I clenched my jaw. "The problem they face is, the old leader is not dead. Just missing."

"Did we snatch him?" It took me a second to realize I

had blurted that out. Not that I would put it past Danika to take matters into her own hands and manhandle a demon just so she could get things her way. I just hoped she was not that dumb.

"Leviathan took charge of the demons a century ago." Danika was looking at me like I was an idiot.

I blinked dumbly. Why were all three of them watching me like they'd never seen me in their life? "What?"

"Leviathan is one of the fallen in charge of Hell," Sissily supplied helpfully, and my mouth formed an "O."

"They can't be touched," I announced stupidly, although everyone in the room knew that. Hell, the humans knew that tidbit, as well.

Even being "other" didn't give us the immunity to be able to touch an angel, fallen or not. We were all happy when the archangels decided to hide in a hole no one could find and wash their hands of the rest of us. The fallen were a different matter, but not less deadly for all, including their demons. Barely-there contact could turn even Danika to ash.

"So, he just ditched the demons? What the actual fuck, Danika? You didn't think that was important for us to know?" It was a day for me to blurt out asinine questions, it seemed. River and Sissily wore matching affronted expressions.

"Watch your language," my grandmother hissed at me.

Like I'd never heard her curse up a storm when she thought no one was around. I was sore, high on whatever herbs they used to dull my pain, and freaked the hell out. Excuse the fuck out of me for using profanities.

"No one knows where Leviathan is, and they've been searching for him for almost a year," she continued after giving me a stern stare down. "And that's not the half of what is happening. The vampire elders are coming out of their stupor, demanding their Council be reassembled so they can have a vote in who does what. Like the rest of us are just the fools who cleaned up the mess they made and will be ready to welcome them with open arms." That last part was muttered more to herself than the rest of us.

Silence fell over us like an anvil around our necks. I felt the weight of it trying to choke me, while everything she said continued to spin through my mind until I felt dizzy from it. A thought occurred to me, and I sucked in a much-needed breath to ask why she was telling us all of this now. I didn't fool myself into thinking all of it was news for Sissily and River, mostly judging by the expressions they sported. Both of them knew parts of it, but not all. I never get to ask because Danika was on the roll and dropping even more bombs without mercy.

"Mr. Blackman, I will ask a favor from you." She avoided my intent gaze, which never boded well for me. "I need you to take Hazel to a location I will give you once we get to my office." River was already nodding like he had the right to make decisions in my name. "You will keep her there until I, and only I tell you to bring her back. Am I clear?"

There was still something Danika wasn't telling us. I could taste it on my tongue but couldn't put my finger on it. All the mumbo-jumbo had a purpose, and that was to distract me. The problem was it was working, damn her.

"Like hell he will." I was out of the bed flashing my ass cheeks at Sissily before River even opened his mouth. "You don't get to tell me where to go." My accusing finger stabbed the air in front of Blondie's nose. "And you"—Whirling on my grandmother, I barely stopped myself from slapping away the look on her face when she raised an eyebrow at me— "don't get to hide me like some eternal sin you don't want anyone finding out about."

My shout would've been more impressive if I didn't sway like a drunken moose, bare ass and all, but whatever. Sissily, the amazing person she was, darted to my back and cinched the hospital gown with fistfuls of fabric. Her good intentions pointed my nipples in Danika's face, which she didn't appreciate going off the grimace twisting her features. River, on the other hand, had no complaints, his gaze leisurely traveling up and down my body until he caught my grandmother's scowl. He had the decency to look ashamed after that.

"I think your grandmother is right, Miss Byrne." Blondie laid it on thick to get back in Danika's good graces, the jerk. "As the last of the Byrne line, you should be protected while things settle down. At least until Leviathan is found."

Taking a wider stance, I crossed my arms and gave him my most impressive bitch face. When Sissily didn't join me, I turned a glare at her over my shoulder. That poked her ass to jump next to me in the same stubborn pose. It was us two against the two of them. There was no chance Danika and River were going to win the stare down.

"No." My chin jutted up a notch.

"Without magic, you are not safe in the middle of all this, Miss Byrne." Oh no he didn't. River didn't just dig his own grave.

"Dude, ouch." Sissily jerked back like he'd insulted her and not me, even though she appeared chagrined when Danika narrowed her gaze. "We all know Hazel turns psycho when you mention her not having magic," my friend mumbled apologetically as a plan formed in my head.

For any of them to ship me anywhere, they'd need to get their hands on me.

"When am I supposed to leave for this place?" At my sweet smile, all of them gaped, Sissily going as far as bending her upper body sideways to give me a better look. "What? You are right. I have no magic, and I'd rather not have more skin melting off my bones, mm-kay? So, when?"

"Best will be on Saturday, late afternoon." Danika's eyes were slits. She was right not to trust me.

"Cool. I'll be ready by then."

They stood frozen while I rummaged through the infirmary room in search of my clothes. My jaw clenched when I lifted the silky blouse between two fingers to see the shredded mess that it was. My pants were not bad, so I stabbed my legs through them, zipping them up before I turned my back to take off the damn gown. Placing the open back to my front, I tied a knot in it to make it a very ugly top, which worked in a pinch, then I padded barefoot to the door.

"I have to go pack," I told the room without looking back. "I'll see you at home, Grandmother."

The magic bubble popped, giving me my escape, and before they could say anything, I was out the door. The moment it closed, I made a mad dash out of there. Let them think I was on my way home.

I pointed my feet straight for the library.

Chapter Twelve

"Out," I hissed at the couple of people I found perusing books like it was a designer shoe sale.

The guy jerked back and his face reddened, but he must've seen the crazy I knew was all over my face so he'd thought better of it. Smart on his part because I was past mental at that time. Snatching the woman's hand, he dragged her out of the library, her outraged protests going faint the further away they moved from the now-closed door. It wasn't the first time I'd been called names, and it wouldn't be the last. I could bet the magic I didn't have on it.

Fists jammed on my hips, I panted, part from anger about River's comment and part from a freak out because Danika wanted to hide me like a pair of dirty underwear. My body rocked back and forth from the strength of my heartbeat, which was drumming against my ribs with a vengeance. I'd be damned if I let them hide me away.

There must be a spell or something in this jungle I was standing in that could help me. While witches hid so they didn't end up burned at the stake or drowned, humans used to dabble in spells, too. Majority of the time, it never worked, but the handful of times it did gave me hope. If a human could do it, so could I.

I just had to find the right one.

Giving the nasty jars a wide berth, I dove in through the rows of bookshelves filled to the brim with texts. Books were nailed hard in every space available, some of them sticking out a couple of inches because they couldn't be jammed in. My trembling hands traced the spines, my gaze darting from one title to the other in search of … I had no idea what. Something. Anything. Halfway through the first row, I stopped, remembering the voice I heard when Alex made me check my intuition that morning. Was it that morning? It felt like it had been a year since I saw the alpha. Only silence met me when I breathed deep and closed my eyes. Intuition my ass.

My mind got sidetracked by that, so when the pain zapped through my arms, it nearly doubled me over. The herbs they used to numb the pain from the demonic magic were wearing off, and I had little time before I was curled up in a ball praying to Hecate to just kill me. My skin prickled with goosebumps remembering the pain from earlier that day. It was a great motivator to light a fire under my now covered behind to push me forward.

It was getting late, too. Deep shadows fell between the rows of books, making it hard to see little less read anything in the darkening library. With a deep sigh, I turned back to flip the light switch that not many used in the building. Soon the candles would come to life with their blue flames that never gave off heat, but that was wasting time I didn't have. The tall, arched windows showed gray skies and lights popping up in windows on the surrounding buildings when I reached for the switch, my fingertips grazing the plastic.

Bright flame burst to life an inch from my face.

On impulse, my hand went from reaching for a light switch right into a fist and shooting forward. The flame died, and a squeak bounced off the library walls when a forearm blocked my attack. But I wasn't done. My foot swept in a circle, turning me around by three hundred and sixty degrees, and I heard the satisfying "Oomph!" when a body smacked the floor. The air whooshed out of whoever had decided to sneak up on me, and they groaned at my feet. All I could make out was the gray outline of a person at that point, so without looking away, I reached out and flipped the switch.

My best friend glowered at me from the floor, her crooked ponytail a separate living being on her head.

"What are you doing here?" My accusing tone only made matters worse.

"Same thing you are doing," Sissily spat at me through her teeth. "I swear, Hazel, one of these days I'm going to fry your ass so bad you'll think twice before getting anywhere near me." Raising from her sprawl, she dusted off her leggings and t-shirt with jerky movements.

"Where is Blondie?"

"On his way to your house to apologize to you for the word vomit." An evil grin split her face. "I even told him which window is yours and advised him to beg forgiveness through it because you'll never open the door."

I barked out a laugh, my shoulders sagging. "You are a mean creature, Sissily. Anyone ever told you that?"

"I learned from the best." She pointed her nose at the ceiling, sniffing at me.

"The student has surpassed the master." We both chortled at that. "Danika?"

"Shadowblood cornered her before she had a chance to escape, so they are locked in her office." My friend shivered in disgust. "I swear if I spent another lifetime around that man, I still wouldn't be able to stand him."

We both agreed on it when it came to our high priest. Shadowblood had this aura around him, especially when I was near, that made our stomachs churn. Since I could remember, not once has he looked at me with anything but contempt or hatred. Why I bothered him so much was not a hard guess, but the reason he hated Sissily was an ongoing mystery. It was more than just her hanging out with me. He was good at pretending in front of Danika, but we'd seen him staring daggers at us more than was called for.

"Girl, same." I shivered just thinking about Shadowblood.

"Did you get a start already?" Sissily got back to business, determination burning in her blue eyes.

"Not really. It was getting pitch black in here." My hand swirled around the light switch. "The first row is out since it's all elemental magic, though. I managed to look through that only."

"You want to start at the back or the front?" Lifting her arms, she took hold of her ponytail and yanked on the strands in hopes of straightening it. It made it more crooked and really puffy, forcing me to eye it critically. "I don't care if it starts talking from my head," she snapped when I pursed my lips.

"It's your hair." Hands up in surrender, I took a step back. "I'll take the back. That way if Danika or River decide to join us, I'll be able to hide."

With a firm nod, Sissily jumped to work with gusto. I

had to duck when I walked around her because she was pulling books off the shelves like she had a personal vendetta against them, her eyebrows pinched low over her eyes. Not for the first time, I thanked whoever found me worthy to give me a friend like her. I personally never thought I deserved her, but I refused to give her back. Sissily Stormblood was one of a kind. She was loyal, strong, caring, and I was grateful to have her in my life.

My bare feet slapped over the smooth stone as I shuffled to the far end of the library. I could barely hear my friend muttering to herself and the smack of books hitting the floor when she dismissed them. With clenched teeth to bare the pain returning with each breath, I mimicked Sissily and started on the dusty books. People rarely came to this end since most of the useful texts were lined closer. Plus, nobody wanted to take a ten-minute walk just to get here. Modern times had even made witches lazy and entitled. We expected everything at our fingertips the moment we needed it and not a second later.

The imprint of my fingers was left on the dust accumulated over the leather, but I sucked it up and dug my way through one row. Most of them were in a language I didn't understand because I didn't find it useful to learn without magic, and the rest were in a dead language no one understood. Well, maybe Danika knew the language, but no one normally did otherwise. No wonder they had two fingers of dust on top of them. I was wasting time looking at freehand drawings made by a toddler who got his hands on a box of crayons, I was sure of it.

"And I am the weirdo with no magic." I snorted under my breath, twisting my head this way and that trying to understand what I was seeing. Hysterical laughter bubbled in my throat when I realized it was a drawing of a penis with ivy twisted around it. What made me choke was the fact it was sitting upright in a chalice like a damn umbrella shoved in a cocktail glass.

"Stop that, Hazel, and get to work," Sissily whisper-yelled from down the row, not lifting her face from the pages she was flipping through.

"It's a penis." My choked snort was much louder that time, and her head whipped in my direction. I raised the book to show her with my fingers spread to hold the page open, my other hand twirling around the drawing like I was a hostess on a game show. "In a cup." A giggle escaped me. "Like an umbrella."

"You're so stupid." But she was biting back a giggle, too. I could see it.

"Would you like a penis in your cocktail, milady?" Butchering a British accent did earn me a straight-out laugh from my friend. "We do have edible and inedible options."

"Very mature, Hazel Byrne. You are pulling off adulthood like no one else." She could say whatever she wanted because the grin was scrunching her eyes.

"I quit adulthood a long time ago. It's boring." Closing the book, I dumped it at my feet to join the other useless ones. "The only time I like it is when they ask for an ID at the bar. I'll deal with it for a drink."

"You and me both, sister." Her tone was absent minded, and I knew I'd lost her.

After that, I really put my back into it and dove through the books with desperation fed by each passing minute. Voices floated through the closed door, forcing us to stop our search and hold our breaths, but luckily no one came. Thoughts of River talking to a closed window tried to pull my focus, but I refused. I needed to stay alive and not shunned by my kind first. I'd think about why

Blondie popped in my head more often than not after that.

Magic bloomed around us, filling the air when our coven mates started and finished their rituals. Hours trickled by slowly and too fast for my liking at the same time. A few times I found myself drifting off, until my head ducked sharply and my body jerked as I gasped awake. Sissily didn't fare better, either, leaning heavily on the bookshelves or crawling on all fours around piles of books on the floor. I could feel dawn approaching like an itch under my skin, and we had nothing to show for it.

All the searching had been for nothing.

"You could try this." Sissily swayed on her feet, her jaw cracked on a wide yawn, and stuck an open grimoire under my nose. Swallowing the scream that lodged in my throat told me I must've fallen asleep. Again.

"Isn't this a call to a deity? A seer would do?" It took quite a bit of blinking to bring the looped scrawl into focus. My eyes were scratchy and dry when I lifted my gaze to her face. "You want me to pull a prophecy out of my ass? Are you insane? They'll kill me if they find out I'm lying."

"Like they can prove all the nonsense the seers spew day and night. Most of it is gibberish anyway." My heart skipped a beat at her slurred words.

I kept it to myself, but in all honesty, I was very superstitious. Especially when it came to seers or prophecies. Maybe because I had no magic and I didn't know if witches really spoke to gods and the Fates or not, it made the whole thing scary as shit for me. If my friend was not so desperate to find a solution to my problem, I was sure she wouldn't be offering something that had a death sentence written all over it.

"Okay." That time the lie tasted like tar on my tongue,

but for her sake, I would've agreed to anything. "I can totally pull off gibberish Hecate herself won't be able to decipher."

"That's the spirit." Sissily shoved the open grimoire into my hands. "Copy the incantation while I go to the cafeteria and grab us some coffee. We won't be able to drive home otherwise." She knew I hated that place, so she offered to do it without making me feel like shit, which I would have if I had to say no.

Her back was already turned when I nodded, and I watched her go until she disappeared from the row of bookshelves. Only then did I release the sigh and let my shoulders slump. Looking through the library was a bust, and for a second, I entertained the idea of making up a prophecy. *Who will know that it's a lie,* a voice prodded my brain.

"I will know, that's who," I mumbled under my breath as I dug my way out of the piles of books around me.

There would be fresh hell to be paid when Danika discovered the mess we made, but on the bright side, the chances of me being cast out were high. Let fucking Sasha Airborne, the bitch, clean it up. The idea of that evil witch stacking books while cursing me to high hell gave me the energy to shuffle my way to the front in search of a pen and paper. Although the cafeteria was on the other side of the building, I knew Sissily would be back in no time.

Just as I was rounding the corner at the edge of the last bookshelf, my shoulder bumped into a line of stacked books protruding from it. It made me stagger, and the grimoire I had in my hands dropped on the floor with a heavy thud. That was followed by another smack when the damn book, which jabbed me in the arm, hit the ground too, falling on the spine, and it flopped open somewhere in the middle. An invisible breeze skirted across my skin, and goosebumps covered my arms. My heart jammed in my windpipe, and I flipped around searching for some asshole with air magic trying to pull a prank on me.

No one was in the library but me.

Dread pooled in my stomach, and I really didn't want to be in the damn room anymore. The first traces of dawn were peeking through the tall windows, casting purples and pinks over the wooden shelves and leather tomes. What little light was poking through the brightening sky pierced the liquid in the jars, giving all the eyeballs, fingers, and such a menacing vibe. I had every intention of snatching the grimoire and hightailing it out of there, but when I bent at the waist to grab it, the text on the opened book got my attention. It was a siren song overtaking my mind.

I was powerless to resist it.

Chapter Thirteen

Lesson 7: *If a book fucks with your brain, run.*

Somewhere in the back of my mind, I knew something was not right. First, what my eyes were seeing and what my brain was translating did not match. I would bet the magic I didn't have that I was reading a language I'd never seen before in my life. And I lived with Danika. That witch had books in so many tongues I was pretty sure some of them were not even in recorded history of any kind. The text was way past dead language. It fell into some alien mumbo-jumbo bullshit.

Second, and most important, alerting me I was in shit up to my eyeballs was the fact that the book was talking to me. Whispering was more like it, but that was semantics. A soothing tone caressed my ears as I leaned eagerly forward like a dumbass. An idiot would run screaming from something like that. Not yours truly. I sat there on my knees gaping like a fool while its voice twisted and curled around me in a lover's embrace.

Then the letters, which I could read mind you, started glowing, the golden tone making them look like they were floating up from the page. My hand lifted, my fingers stretching in an attempt to touch them and see if they were real. I should've used the other hand, the one without a pentagram tattoo marking me as a witch, but like everything else in my life, I never did what was smart.

The tops of my fingers grazed the floating golden words, and for a moment, I nearly convinced myself that I must've fallen asleep and was dreaming. My tense muscles unlocked with the thought, and my fingers sank into the golden light. Phrases like "Finally, it has been so long," and "How dare they lock us," exploded in my head, almost knocking me to my side. The light crawled up my hand until it reached my wrist while I stared at it unblinking, not able to do anything but suck in short, gasped breaths. I had the mind to start freaking out when the bandages wrapped all over my arms from wrist to shoulder loosened and fell to the floor in a neat pile.

Anger hissed from the soothing voice overtaking my mind when the glow inched up my still blistered skin, the color changing from golden to mint green. It was such a pretty shade that I gazed at it dreamily for a long moment before I pulled myself out of the hypnotic daze with a shake of my head. A chill was sinking under my skin where heat had scorched it a second ago. Right before my eyes, my arm healed, the angry red tone disappearing as soon as the glow reached it. My pointer finger itched like a bitch, and I barely prevented myself from taking my teeth to it.

I knew I needed to get away from the light and the voice. Hell, I needed to burn the damn book if the cursed thing thought it could take over someone's mind, but all I could do was blink and gasp. When the crisp open pages touched my cheek, I realized I was plastered on the floor with my face on top of the book. I felt so tired. More than before when I dozed off a few times deep in the belly of the library. Maybe if I took a few minutes to rest, I would be able to fight whatever the cursed thing was doing to me. I was sure of it.

A chuckle bounced around my skull, snapping my eyes open.

"I'm ... going ... kick ... ass." My threat was slurred, something not even a dozen drinks had managed to force out of me while I played roadkill on the library floor. Where in Hecate's name was Sissily?

"For waking you up?" The whisper was clearer but neither male nor female. It was many voices speaking from both genders, which turned it into an echoing buzz. "For giving you back what was taken from you, child. Is that why you fight us?"

The chill was crawling up my other arm, and I had no need to see it to know the skin was healing. With every blister healed, my skin tightening until it felt like my bones were being squeezed in a vice. Lungs burning from the inability to inflate as much as I needed, I sipped air through barely open lips.

This was how I died.

On the floor like some pathetic scum in the middle of the coven building.

Dressed in a hospital gown pretending to be a top, and pants crusted from demon blood.

Barefoot.

Rage erupted in my chest, a bubbling volcano spitting and hissing like a sentient being. If I was going to kick the bucket, I was going to do it on my terms. Dressed to the nines with my favorite shoes on, damn it. Not with bare feet and chunks of hair missing from my head.

"You will not kill me." It hurt to speak. "Let. Me. Go."

"So strong," the voice purred in pleasure. "Such a strong mind. Iron will."

"Fuck you." That one cost me because I bit my tongue and blood flooded my mouth.

I learned that if some magical entity is trying to kill your ass, you should just keep your mouth shut and let it have at it. Definitely not something I practiced, keeping the trap shut, but solid advice, nonetheless. As I was gulping my own life fluid, I found it important to point that out to myself, just in case it was wisdom I could take with me to the next life, or afterlife. Whatever was waiting for me on the other side, in any case.

I was going insane.

Instead of fighting to stay alive, I was having conversations in my head about wisdom and afterlife. The rage was still skin deep, so I reached for it and used it to fight the control the entity had over my limbs. I could've shouted in victory when I lifted my shaking body on my hands and knees, blood dribbling down my chin. Fat drops hit the open pages of the book, splattering and staining the cream paper. Before my blurry eyes, the blood disappeared, sinking into the words like the cursed things were lapping it up. My mind was screaming shit on repeat when the whispers abruptly stopped. I'd never heard a silence so loud in my life.

And then it laughed.

A joyful, beautiful sound that froze my attempts to crawl away from it. It was impossible that something so beautiful but made my chest hurt could be evil, right? Terror ripped through me when I found myself smiling from ear to ear while blood dribbled down my chin, and my limbs shook hard enough to rattle my teeth.

"Yessss." I'm not ashamed to say I peed a little when the voice hissed in triumph like a venomous snake. I might be a stubborn mule, but when my bladder gave up on me, I was out. "Now we bond."

The hold on my body vanished, and I crumbled in a heap, my hip taking the brunt of it along with my thick skull. I deserved the knock to the head for being in the library in the first place, though I didn't appreciate it at the time.

"Wait," I squeaked like a mouse, which pissed me off. "Bond? No," I barked.

"Yessss." Another hiss had me scrambling away from the cursed thing, crab-walking the hell out of its reach.

"You are losing your mind, Hazel. Books don't talk." I wished there was more conviction in my tone, but I wasn't going to nitpick.

The book in question was sitting open still, quiet, not at all chatty, and unassuming. I was eyeing it like a snake in the grass while I waited for it to pounce. When minutes passed and all I did was watch it unblinking, my locked muscles relaxed. I was hallucinating. That was the best explanation for what happened. Too much espresso, no sleep, a fight with not one but two demons, and stress would make anyone snap. The pep talk helped to unfreeze the rest of me, and I plopped heavily on my tailbone. If I wasn't numb from fear all over, it would've hurt.

Wiping the blood painting my chin with the back of my hand, I grimaced when I saw how much of it was there. My tongue wiggled in my mouth to check if I bit through it, but apart from the sting on the left side, I didn't have any pain. I gave up on cleaning my face and gingerly crawled back toward the book. The thought of me hallucinating was firmly at the front of my mind like a shield. Or maybe Rakshasa magic made me imagine things since it burned me. If it had longer-lasting effects, it would be totally possible. By the time I was poised above the open pages I had myself convinced.

A bright light like someone turned a flashlight on an inch from my retinas blasted me in the face, throwing my body backward. The back of my head made a sickening crunch when it smacked the stone like a melon, bouncing on it a few times. My mouth was open in a scream, but no sound came out of it. All the shrieking was done internally where it felt like my body was being ripped apart on a molecular level. Waves of scorching heat washed over me from head to toe, followed by a current of ice that made me wish for death that never came. My organs were melting, turning into puddles before reforming and regrowing themselves.

Through it all, I was locked inside a tiny box in my psyche, held prisoner in my own body, and forced to watch the torture in explicit detail. I flopped around like a fish out of water, seizures raking me one after another. My eyes rolled to the back of my head, but that didn't prevent me from seeing it all, the bastard who did this to me making sure I had an out-of-body experience and a front-row seat. The pain was something I'd never felt, and it was so much that at one point it didn't hurt at all. Seeing what was probably my last moments of life didn't scare me anymore.

Nor did the dark stain forming around my head like a halo.

After a lifetime, or maybe a blink of an eye, my body went still and I was sucked back into it like an elastic band snapping. My awareness slammed inside my meat suit, and I gasped, filling my lungs with so much air it made me cough hard enough to puncture a lung. Hacking and spitting, I rolled on my knees and stumbled to my feet. Hand pressed on the bookshelf to keep my balance, my other hand reached for the back of my head to see how deep the gash was. Halfway up my arm, I froze and stared at my skin, my jaw hitting my chest.

Sigils lit by some inner glow I did not possess before the cursed book sunk its clutches in me blinked in and out of existence. The symbols flickered and died only to be replaced with others, all of them with a faint, deep golden glow just like the words of the book when they came to life. My stomach dropped to my feet, and I couldn't even swallow from the tightness in my throat. A distant laughter rekindled my rage, and my head whipped around to search for it. Again, I was alone, and the book was silent a couple of feet away from me. It took effort to realize where the laughter was coming from.

It was me.

I was laughing like a crazy woman, deep belly guffaws that shook my shoulders. Tears streaked down my cheeks, and still I chortled, unable to stop. When a stitch developed in my side and I didn't stop, fear stabbed me that the torture was not over. Maybe I would laugh myself to death.

Talk about irony.

For someone who barely smiled, it was quite fitting to kill them by way of laughter. Wasn't it?

The library door opening sounded like a bullet being fired in a closed room.

The hinges were too loud, and the air rushing in through the barely formed crack pelted my overheated skin, which still flickered with strange sigils. Every sense was amplified, overwhelming me to the point I couldn't see which way was up and which down. The fear I pushed down after the book released its hold reared its head, and something foreign and powerful enough to steal my breath burst out of me. My arm flicked to the side in a wide arc, slicing the air, and a cloud of light exploded from my fingertips.

I screamed.

My shriek was drowned by the impact of the magic with the barely opened door, and whoever was trying to enter had tonsils of steel judging by the strength of their shout. Panic was strangling me that Danika would walk through the damn door and she would see me lit up like a damn Christmas tree in the middle of her library. I had no idea what was happening to me, but I sure as fuck didn't want her to know about it.

The ground under my bare feet started shaking.

Panting like a feral animal, I realized one thing. The higher my fear climbed, the stronger the quaking of the ground became. The problem was, I couldn't stop it.

I couldn't stop any of it.

One, because I had no idea what was going on.

Two, I was freaked the hell out and in shock.

Glass crackled behind me, and I spun around to watch cracks spider web all over the windows. And the building kept rocking while books spilled from the floor-to-ceiling shelves like a waterfall. Someone was calling my name, but the voice was faint and easily ignored.

In the middle of it all, I still laughed.

Lines zigzagged under my feet, splitting the stone in random asymmetric patterns. The voice that kept calling my name was joined by others, all of them shouting. That didn't make things worse, but it didn't calm them either.

Then they used magic to enter the library.

Whatever monster I had in me lost its shit when magic

prodded the air around me. It all happened so fast that I had no time to prepare or brace for impact. Puffs of frosted air clouded in front of my face the same way they did in the middle of the winter. My galloping heartbeat slowed, and a sense of calm washed over me, erasing the trembling of my limbs. It was like the earth itself was holding its breath for a long, suspenseful moment.

Magic exploded out of the center of my chest, bursting windows, walls, and the domed ceiling above me, spraying it outward. All the books bloomed in bright flames, filling the air with ash and floating cinders while my hair whipped around my face on an invisible blast of wind. One second, the magic was exiting my body, and the next, it snapped right back in, and then I sailed through the air, taking broken parts of obsidian walls with me as I flew.

I was dumped in the middle of a destroyed office where, by some miracle, the large desk had survived. I recognized it immediately when my eyes uncrossed from the impact a second before Sissily materialized next to me from out of thin air. My ears were ringing, and I could only watch her mouth move because I couldn't hear a word she said.

"What in the Hecate's name did you do, stupid girl." Shadowblood's snarl of indignation was the first to pierce the thudding in my ears. It figured I would end up on my ass in his damn office, boobs out and pants ripped to resemble hot pants that barely covered my ass.

"Oh, shut up, Shadowblood," I hissed at him, covering my chest as well as I could with one arm. At least I could make a dash for it before Danika found me.

"Hazel Byrne," my grandmother gasped from somewhere, and I buried my face in my hands.

I was royally screwed.

Chapter Fourteen

"Anything we can salvage?" my grandmother asked, but I could tell by her tone she didn't expect it, though she hoped for it nonetheless.

River shook his head and wouldn't meet her gaze as he weaved his way to a pile of debris he used as a chair. We all did the same when Danika marched us to what was left of her office. Shadowblood had stuttered accusations when my grandmother found me playing with a half-naked glow stick in the middle of the high priest's office, until a part of the domed ceiling dropped on top of him—I swear I had nothing to do with it ... I think—and no one was sure if he would wake up from the coma or not. As much as I disliked the old witch, I didn't wish him death, although Danika didn't seem bothered by his vegetative state at the time.

The coven building was ... a mess. Those looking in from the outside were left speechless, while humans on their news screamed about meteors hitting Cleveland and gods punishing us for daring to use their powers. I had no energy to worry about their stupidities because for the last couple of hours, Danika had been my judge and jury.

First, she yelled, something she rarely did on principle because she had a gift for drilling her point without raising her voice. Seeing my grandmother lose her cool was not something I thought I'd experience in my lifetime, so it kept me silent. While she barked very loudly at me for being childish, reckless, and plain stupid, to which I had nothing to say since it was all true, her gaze kept flicking to the blinking sigils on my exposed skin, and each time she saw them, her face lost more of its color.

Danika raged for a long time, and that was the reason most of our coven mates bolted as far away from the destroyed building as they could. When only a handful stayed to try and clean up some of the mess, River decided to join us, drilling my skull with his intent stare, which I of course avoided like the plague. As soon as he joined us, my grandmother asked him to do the silent spell, and we ended up squatting in her broken office ever since.

"What in the goddess name are you smiling about?" Danika's incredulous tone snapped me out of my thoughts.

"Nofin.'" It came out muffled. I was biting my cheeks on the inside, mortified when I realized I had a huge grin plastered on my face.

"It better be nothing, Hazel, or so Hecate help me, I will skin you where you stand." My mouth opened to tell her I didn't appreciate her yelling at me when I didn't do anything on purpose, but her murderous glare glued my lips shut. "With my bare hands." Danika snarled at me. Snarled!

"This was not Hazel's fault." Sissily tightened her arms around me where she'd been hugging me ever since she found me in Shadowblood's office. "I was with her all night and went to get coffee. That was ten minutes max she was alone in the library. No one could do that much damage in such a short time."

If anything, Danika looked more pissed.

"Honest," my best friend continued, undeterred by the scowl aimed at her. "And she has no magic. This is the work of a witch. Someone put a spell on her. On your granddaughter." Sissily stressed that tidbit. "You should hunt them down instead of yelling at her. She's been through so much."

My lips folded on their own while I attempted to bite back a laugh. Bless Sissily and her undying loyalty. My best friend was ready to bite Danika's head off for me, and in the middle of the disaster that was my life, warmth spread through my chest. Before guilt stabbed me. Would she defend me the same when she found out what I did? That my stupidity was the reason I was a magical glow stick she held in an embrace?

The sigh coming from my grandmother was heavy enough to ruffle the short hairs that curled around my face. She pressed her fingers to the bridge of her nose and squeezed her eyes shut, no doubt praying to Hecate for patience. River's eyes were locked on me, not that they'd stayed away for longer than a second, but I watched Danika with rapt attention.

"What does this mean?" Flinching from the husky, strange tone in my voice, I swallowed the bile burning my throat.

When Danika opened her eyes, her emerald irises swirled with an emotion I couldn't name. It only pushed the acid of my stomach further up to the roof of my mouth. I'd never seen lines on her face, her skin seeming airbrushed at all times of day or night, but they were there now. For the first time, my grandmother looked tired to the marrow of her bones, showing her age.

"It means everything I did, all the deals I made to protect you are null and void. All for nothing." Her hand reached up to tuck the silky hair away from her face, and my heart stuttered to a stop seeing it shake.

It was fear.

The emotion swirling in those emerald depths was fear, and that more than anything else made me regret every goddess forsaken day of my whole life. I wanted to throw myself at her feet and beg her to forgive me. I wished I had the power to turn back time and never step foot in the library. At one moment, I dared to wish the Rakshasa had killed me and the whole thing was my personal hell instead of real.

"You need to be more specific." Blondie finally lost interest in staring me down, turning his peepers on Danika. "What deals? And why does she keep glowing? Can you glamour her skin before she announces it to the world she is brimming with ancient powers?"

"*We* can see it, Mr. Blackman, but no one else can. I made sure of that. For the last time, I will ask you to stop telling me how to do my job or how to protect my granddaughter."

"What does he mean by brimming with ancient power?" They were free to do a dick measuring contest—I bet Danika had bigger balls by far—some other time. "This whole glowy thing"—I shook my arm like that would rid me of the blinking sigils under my skin— "is because the cursed book blasted me in the face. You know, like when you fall asleep with your face on top of the newspaper and the letters transfer to your cheek? It'll wash off with time, right?"

Silence was my answer.

"I have no magic," I blurted out angrily.

"When you were born, Hazel, your mother …" Danika started leaning back and straightening her spine. I panicked.

"Fuck no, you don't." Seething, I wiggled out of the death grip Sissily had on me. "Don't you dare start some bullshit fairytale now, Grandmother. I couldn't care less about the time I was born. What I do care about, however, is removing this creepy stuff from my skin, mm-kay?"

"Sit down, Hazel Byrne, and keep your mouth shut," Danika snapped, and my knees gave out. I plopped next to my best friend like I was a puppet and my grandmother had cut my strings.

"I don't want to hear it." Sounding like a petulant child, I begged her with my eyes. She never fell for the whole puppy dog look, but it was worth a try as a last-ditch effort.

"Your mother died to save your life." As was Danika's way, she was brutal in her honesty, not caring one bit that my heart was grinding into dust with her every word. "Your body was too weak for the amount of magic Hecate bestowed on you, and your heart kept giving up. My daughter used the last drops of her life and soul to help me contain it, block it, if you will, until you were much older and could learn to expel the access in non-harmful ways, but it was not enough." My grandmother's eyes were distant, unfocused, taking her to times long past where I had no right to be. Not if what she was saying was true.

"Desperate to at least keep one of you with me, I went to look for Michael." Danika gulped, and Sissily gasped. "I couldn't find the archangel, not in time anyway." I knew what she would say next before it was spoken out loud. "I turned to Leviathan next. He didn't want to help at first, but after I said he couldn't name a price I was not willing to pay, he made me a deal. I accepted, and that day he sealed your magic. No one but the fallen himself could unlock the binding, not even me."

"You made a deal with the devil." The ground shook under us, and when I breathed to calm down, it took a second to hear Sissily shushing me like I was a babe while she was rubbing my arm. "Great. Next thing you know, I'll need to be burped so I don't blow up the town."

"I'll take that responsibility." River smirked at my frustration, and without conscious thought, I flicked my wrist at him.

Sissily and I both jumped to our feet and rushed to him when his body was flung through the air and slammed on the dirty floor. It would've been comical to see him flopping around like a sock monkey by an invisible toddler having a tantrum if I was not the one hurting him unintentionally. He groaned and scowled at me when I helped him up. I was grateful to Sissily for giving me her t-shirt and prancing around in her bra when River's head came level with my free-styling boobs.

"Sorry, I didn't mean to do that," I mumbled, yanking him to his feet and releasing him just as fast.

Luckily, Blondie had other things on his mind. "That's why you wanted me to hide her. You can't find Leviathan."

"No one can find the fallen," Danika huffed, a muscle spasming in her jaw. "Which brings me to now. Nothing, no book, no demon, witch, angel, or Fae could unseal Hazel's magic. No one but Leviathan and me should know she even had it. So, how did this happen?" She was looking at me, so I racked my brain for any details I could've missed.

"It was a book we confiscated from the Kisha demon, along with the body parts," I supplied helpfully. "Or I think it was since it was jammed in the shelf along with them." Danika kept those unnerving peepers on my face. "What? I didn't want to touch it. Hell, Sissily and I catalogued them, and it didn't say shit to me then. This morning it became chatty Cathy."

"Say something," I begged when I couldn't handle her silence anymore. "Hang on a second. What did Leviathan ask for when you made a deal?"

"Now you start asking the right kind of questions." I nearly fainted when pride shone in her emerald gaze. Danika never looked at me like that. Never.

It scared the shit out of me.

"Are you dying?" Blurting out the first thing on one's mind was never a good idea.

River groaned as if pained.

"I am not dying." My grandmother rolled her eyes in her classy way so you couldn't even be angry when she did it. "I did, however, promise him my soul in exchange for his help."

"You cannot possibly be that hungry for power. Are you crazy? Your soul?" My voice rose with each question. "No magic is worth your soul."

"Not magic, your life," she told me, her voice so quiet I barely heard her.

"It was my magic you wanted sealed." My accusation hung between us until she smiled at me indulgently.

"The magic was killing you, Hazel. It was stopping your heart. Your mother syphoned as much as she could before I arrived, but the moment she breathed her last breath, it rushed back to you, along with hers. I traded my soul so you could live."

Sobs rocked me where I stood when I thought it was a great idea to yell at her. Sharp pieces of broken obsidian cut into the skin of my knees, and I doubled over until my forehead was pressed down, too. Sissily tried to lift me but couldn't because the tremors raking me shook her off me. Rock and soil groaned at the guilt and pain blasting inside me. Strong arms wrapped around my body, and I was airborne before I stalled over muscled thighs.

River's magic and his cologne washed over me, soothing me like nothing else at that moment. He was muttering sweet nothings in my ear, his hand rasping gently up and down my back. My soot-covered face left patches of dried blood and dirt on his shirt, and he didn't seem to care.

"I'm a parasite." Hiccupping breaths rocked both River and me when I spoke. "A leech. I killed … I killed my mother and Danika …" Ugly crying, I couldn't continue for a while. "Danika promised her soul to Hell for me, too. You should've let me die."

"Nonsense." For the life of me, I didn't understand why my grandmother was smiling.

All the times I dared to imagine a time where I had magic, finding out my mother had died trying to save me and my grandmother had signed over her soul had never crossed my mind. A thought occurred to me.

"You think something, or someone"—My hand sliced the air in front of my throat, mimicking cutting it—"Leviathan? Maybe that's why this happened."

"Short of an archangel or another fallen, nothing could get near him," Danika mused. "He is not dead, I'm sure of it. If he was going down, he would've taken me with him." She might've sounded like she didn't care, but I shivered in River's arms.

"Why did he want your soul that much? Couldn't he ask

for something else? Weren't you worried he could've asked for the souls of the entire coven?"

"All the covens in the world are not worth as much as a soul from a Byrne witch, dear." Danika licked her lips, and my spine snapped straight. More secrets, I could practically smell them. I wouldn't have felt River stiffen if I wasn't sitting on his lap, but I ignored that for the moment.

"Why? Don't get me wrong, I know you are the strongest witch they have, but why are Byrne witches so important?" Sissily took my fingers in hers, offering her support when I was ready to break. I didn't see her move closer to where River held me like a child curled on his chest.

"Because our magic is different from everyone else's." Her pointed look told me not to keep asking. As if that had stopped me before.

"How different? Am I going to turn psycho now and kill indiscriminately?" It was a great possibility that didn't occur to me before. Shadowblood being knocked out by a piece of falling ceiling played on repeat. "Dear goddess, I will, won't I?"

"Stop acting like a child, Hazel, and get a hold of yourself. You are not an animal. You are a witch." All the times I'd wished for her to call me a witch, and now that she did, it felt sour somehow. "Let us be thankful that no one else apart from us present and Shadowblood saw your magic manifesting. I will deal with the High Priest when he wakes up." I could've sworn I heard her mutter, "If he ever wakes up," but that would be insane. Wouldn't it?

"Ummm." River's hum of uncertainty made all of us turn to him at the same time. "I believe one of the Airborne witches was standing in the hallway staring at Hazel when I arrived. It totally slipped my mind until you said that."

"Sasha," Sissily and I growled the name as one.

"We need to find her at once." Danika jumped to her feet, but I didn't bother to move.

If Sasha saw my glow-stick impersonation, I would bet my life half the world knew it, too.

How bad could it be?

Chapter Fifteen

I won the battle of wills and convinced the three stooges we all needed a shower and a change of clothes. Food and rest were optional, and they were fast to dismiss both. Much to my chagrin, River also came to my house—well Danika's if we were into semantics—announcing he would not let any of us out of his sight. When my grandmother pinned him with a glare capable of peeling paint off drywall, he had the decency to blush, something I found adorable.

It only made me want to frustrate him more for some reason.

Since we were not splitting up—Danika's orders—until we were sure Sasha had grown a conscience or a personality in the last how many hours none of us had seen her, I won the battle of being the driver, too. River was the most agreeable on that one, followed by Danika, who thought it smart to remind me long lived and immortal were two very different things, and I should maybe lay off the gas a little. Sissily was the loudest and most vicious advocate of anyone else driving but me. Which of course made me zigzag through traffic like a mad woman, while my best friend tried to drill a hole in the floor of my car by slamming her foot on an invisible break.

I grinned the entire way home.

Shower and changing were done fast and methodically, no one saying a word as we passed each other in the hallway, the three of us with turbans of terry cloth wrapped around our heads and River shirtless with a towel clinging low on his narrow hips. I bet the jerk did that on purpose too, and I cursed up a storm when I tripped on nothing, nearly face planting in the middle of the hallway. I'd walked it my whole life barefoot and on six-inch nail-thin heels, yet that was the first time I stumbled. It wasn't one of my finest moments by a long shot.

What irked me was the fact that Blondie could conjure clothing out of his ass—well, thin air, since we had no male clothing anywhere in our home—yet he had fresh-pressed dress pants and a button-down shirt to match the color of his eyes replacing the towel. When I found myself missing the wet terrycloth that used to cover his ass from my greedy eyes, I announced a little too loudly that it was time to jet.

Unfortunately, makeup, as good as it might be, couldn't hide the fact that me and my best friend were suffering from a major lack of sleep. Sissily had a death wish and was sucking on a coffee, but I needed something much stronger than caffeine. All my hopes and dreams were crushed when I swiped a bottle of tequila from the kitchen in passing. The three of them dove for me from all sides like I was a witch of old trying to steal their firstborn. No amount of grumbling or threats worked to get the booze back, so I gave up on the idea, albeit begrudgingly. To pay them back, I proceeded to flex my arms—more like wiggle my boobs at them—pretending to throw the blinking sigils at their heads.

Only the first time worked, each of them ducking or covering their head.

Danika was not impressed, I'd say that much.

By the time we started making the rounds in search of Sasha, I accidentally busted a hole a quarter of an inch away from Sissily's foot in the car, scorched River's shirt sleeve, and caught Danika's hair on fire. My excessive apologizing didn't make me feel better at all, although all of them reassured me it was not my fault.

It wasn't, but I still felt like a jerk.

"How long until I can control this damn thing?" Maybe asking for the umpteenth time would deliver a different answer. It didn't.

"It'll take practice and a lot of focus," my grandmother said through her teeth when I took the turn too sharp, the tires squealing down the street.

"So, a week tops." It could've been worse, I guessed.

"Where are you going? The house we are visiting is in the other direction." Danika twisted to look behind us like that would give her an answer. "You are going downtown." It was an accusation.

"I'm going to get us some food because my stomach is eating itself." No one applauded me when I parked like a race-car driver in one go. "You can all wait here. I'll be two minutes max."

Four doors slammed shut instead of just mine when I stepped on the curb. Three pairs of eyes dared me to bitch about it. The whole follow-the-leader tactic was going to get old real fast, I just knew it, but I bit down my protests and seethed all the way to the pastry shop and through the line at the counter. My anger evaporated when a tendril of bright light zapped from my finger, flinging a chair across the shop. River pretended like he stumbled on it so they didn't notice the idiot unable to control her magic.

To make me feel more like shit, seven women of all ages rushed to help him right himself, although he was planted like an oak on both feet. Sissily stuffed a sample of some pastry in my mouth to prevent me from making an asinine comment. Blondie flashed me a smile at that, and I chewed the flaky dough like a cow on a mission. Until Danika stabbed me in the side with her pointed, well-manicured nail.

River chuckled the entire time.

Twenty minutes later, I felt less bitchy and more like my old self. Hangry was a real thing, so after stuffing my face until I couldn't breathe anymore. Even I noticed I was more pleasant to be around.

"The place we are going is her uncle's house?" My attempt to break the silence was short lived.

"Yes, on her mother's side," my grandmother answered, but I could tell she was distracted.

Sissily snatched shorts and a tank top from my closet, which worked on her shorter body better than anything else of mine. I kept myself entertained in the quiet car, yanking a pair of leather pants and a corset top to spite Blondie for prancing around my house wearing only a towel. Danika and he, however, looked like royalty on their way to a business meeting, perfectly put together. My best friend and I at least brushed our hair, so we had that going for us. Plus, my newly formed glowing decorations all over my skin.

Distantly, I was aware that I did everything just so I didn't think about it. If I didn't keep my mind busy, there'd be an opening for a freak-out session, and no one wanted to see that. Me being blunt and snarky on the best of days was hard to deal with. Me in a full-on freak-out mode was a nightmare, even to myself. So, I scrutinized the people with me, muttered at idiots driving too slow or too fast—like I was one to talk—and drove. When I couldn't handle the anxiety filling up the car any longer, my gaze found Danika in the rearview mirror.

"What's going on?"

A small smile quirked the corners of her mouth, and she breathed a sigh. "I believe we are being followed."

That put all of us on alert.

"The silver Honda on your right." My eyes locked on the unassuming car in the mirror sticking out on Sissily's side. "They are keeping the same distance since we left the pastry shop." Danika didn't sound accusing, but guilt stabbed me anyway.

"What are the odds of them going in the same direction unrelated to us?" my friend muttered, pretending to check her eyeliner so she could get a better look. "Something is not right with that car."

"I don't want to turn and make it obvious we know what they're up to." My grandmother squirmed in the back seat. "Hazel, you need to buy a larger vehicle instead of this sardine can."

"Let's not insult my car, mm-kay?" My hand patted the steering wheel lovingly. "She is perfect. Yes, you are, don't listen to the mean witch."

River snorted, then coughed to cover it up.

I bared my teeth at him in the rearview mirror.

"Well peeps, hold onto your breaches because we are about to hit warp speed." Wiggling to press my back further into my leather seat, I ignored Sissily's threats of dismemberment if I dared speed up.

Pedal to the metal, everyone slammed back into their seats, and we zoomed down the street at top speed. Our surroundings blurred while my grandmother mumbled a protection spell that wrapped around the car. If the driver of the silver Honda didn't find his gas pedal too, I would've been insulted.

We faced the problem of having a car chase in a residential part of town where the speed limit was thirty-five at best. Not many humans were out, but one of them was one too many for my piece of mind. My car fishtailed when I took a sharp turn left with an immediate right, praying to Hecate to guide me further away from the family homes with white-picket fences and toys sprinkled in their front yards. Strings of very colorful curses spilled from my lips when the jerk in the Honda rammed my car from behind. Sissily screamed loud enough to bust my eardrum.

My friend's comment about something being wrong with the car chasing us became apparent now that it was close enough. Short of climbing on top of my Mercedes, it couldn't be closer if it tried. The windows of the Honda had glamour, preventing anyone from seeing who was inside. My jaw clenched hard enough to crack my teeth. The car swiveled left and right when the road under us trembled, answering my anger.

"Hazel, calm yourself or you will kill us all," Danika barked at me. "Not even a witch can heal a broken neck or a cut-off head."

My head bobbed as I nodded, sucking in deep breaths and blowing them out slowly. My arms were a lightshow fit for the fourth of July with all the light I was giving off. Just as I came down from my tipping point, the Honda slammed our back harder. Shards of glass rained over River and my grandmother, the impact shattering the window. Blondie gave up all pretenses and flipped on his knees to face the jerks.

"It's not even a Honda." River pushed through his teeth. "It's a glamour over an SUV is my guess. No way a Honda can do this much damage."

My brain stuck on the word damage, and my vision bathed in red. I saw the flames coming from River hitting the silver car that was riding our ass. His magic made an impact, but it only forced the spell hiding the real vehicle to flicker, not causing any real damage for them. He kept at it, aiming the streams of flames to hit from different angles while I desperately searched for somewhere to stop. "They have protection, too," I told Sissily. "River can't get a decent hit."

That was all it took for her to crawl over the armrest and squeeze herself between Danika and River. Her ropes of electricity joined the flames, uncaring at that point who saw the magic. Staying alive was more important than humans freaking out at the light show. Air whooshed out of me when the road spat us out on a long stretch of highway with corn fields on either side. With a firm grip on the steering wheel, I jerked to the right, the car plowing through husks until the front wheels dipped into a ditch and we jumped up and down harshly. I killed the engine, yanking on the seatbelt to scramble out. River and Sissily were next to me before I blinked.

"I will go get help." Danika glided out without a hair out of place and gave me a stern look. "Don't die." The next moment she was gone, and I stared dumbly at the empty space she'd occupied a second ago.

"Can she do that?" The shrill sound of my voice didn't bother me one bit. "She's gone." Announcing it to no one in particular, I pointed too. "Can she do that?"

"Here they come," River muttered, and I forgot all about Danika vanishing into thin air. What other secrets had she never shared with me? Why wasn't Sissily surprised as much as I was? Did all of them have the ability to poof out of somewhere? Could I, now that I had magic too?

It all swirled in my brain, making me dizzy, but three jerks the size of bulls on steroids were stomping our way. If I had to take a stab at it, I'd say shifters, but that didn't make sense. Why would Alex send his wolves to attack me? Kill me was more like it, because they had murder written all over them.

A phone chimed in the pregnant silence.

River fished it out of his pocket like we didn't have three psychos coming at us. Whatever he saw, it was like a dark cloud falling over his face.

"Wanna share with the rest of the group?" I chirped, swallowing the hysterical laughter trying to escape from me.

"A video of your glowing skin along with the destroyed building circulated the supernatural network." His gaze zeroed in on my owlish stare, and I didn't like what I saw there. "There is a price on your head. Brought in alive for a payment in full."

"Fuck a duck," Sissily breathed at the same time I whimpered.

I could give the magic back, right?

Right?

Chapter Sixteen

"I seriously don't understand why Danika didn't just, you know"—My hand swirled, indicating the empty place where my grandmother stood moments ago— "make us all poof or something."

The shifters took their sweet-ass time stalking in our direction from across the street where a large military-style SUV was parked on the side of the road instead of the silver Honda that was chasing us. My assumption was they were trying to keep us shaking in our boots, prolonging our impending doom. Although neither one of my companions showed an ounce of fear. If anything, River and Sissily appeared bored out of their minds, even with me shifting from foot to foot like a two-year-old who needed to pee.

"She can only transport herself, and even that is a very unusual gift for a witch." Something in Sissily's tone made me peel my gaze from our pursuers so I could look at her. "Sifting is a Fae trait, none of the "other" can replicate it."

"It figures Danika can." My petulant muttering earned me a chuckle from River.

"Your grandmother is very powerful." It was like Blondie thought I didn't know he was an idiot. "And has a lot of secrets."

"Can we just not worry about Danika right now and, I don't know, run?" The pastry I ate in the car was souring in my stomach, and I totally was ready to give it to the corn field as a liquid offering.

"We are not running from shifters." I didn't want to remind River that we were actually, indeed, running while pointing at my totaled Mercedes behind us with its nose in the field, but I didn't want to be *that* person. The poor thing was like an Emu sticking its head in the soil, and for about two seconds, I debated joining it.

"Give us the witch and we will let you go," the shifter on the left called out when they were almost close enough for me to see their eyes glowing, their animal close to the surface.

"Which one?" Sissily sassed, while I was trying to unglue the tongue from the roof of my mouth. "There are three witches here, but I'd say from the look of y'all, you can't handle any of us."

It took some time for my brain to quit panicking and pull some important information from things I did know about shifters. In my defense, I went from under a truck to being pushed through a grinder, my body melted from the inside out and put back together, and I was now the perfect example of a glow stick, all in less than twelve hours. The fact that I could think at all was nothing short of a miracle. But I did remember the most important thing about shifters.

They had no magic.

Well, if you take into consideration their body shifting into an animal, I supposed they did, but not active magic they could use against us in a fight. Since Sissily struck a nerve with her sweet smile and snark, all three of them had their lips curled over their teeth in a snarl while they seemingly doubled in size before our eyes. My skin warmed, the sigils pulsed brighter in reaction to my emotional state, and my eyes jerked from my arms to the three shifters. None of them reacted to it, reminding me Danika had placed a glamour on me.

A wide grin stretched my mouth from ear to ear.

"Girl, you look like a psycho when you smile," Sissily mumbled from the side of her mouth, not moving her lips.

Spreading out to corner us from three sides, the shifters were done playing. "Last chance." Their leader, I guessed, snarled, dismissing me and my friend, his gaze locked on River. "Hand over the brunette, and you walk away unharmed."

"Hercules called, and he wants his muscles back," I blurted loud enough to have his peepers on me. "How about you take your big dick energy and go lift something, mm-kay? Let those of us with a brain do what we do best. Like, let's say, use our heads for more than just an accessory."

"Dayuummnnn." My friend was all over that like white on rice. "Burn, bitch." Sissily had electrical currents jumping between her fingers.

All three shifters pounced, their bodies twisting and changing shape midair. It would've been beautiful to watch if their main focus wasn't snatching me so they could get a paycheck. The wolves, larger than the natural animal with their heads at about shoulder level on me, landed in the flattened part of the field where we stood. Saliva dribbled from their snapping jaws, stretching nearly to their chests before splattering on the soil. What took me by surprise was the black color of their fur. If I remembered correctly, Alex once said his entire pack was known as the grey wolves, hence his family name Greywood.

Magic crackled in the air around us, lifting the hairs on my arms at attention. River raised his arms and started spinning flames above his head before throwing them at the closest wolf. His full lips never for a second stopped moving as he called on his element to come to his aid. The shifter howled in pain when his fur caught on fire, and then he rolled around in an attempt to extinguish it. If I didn't have just as large of a shifter circling me in hopes to find the best way to snatch me, I would've loved to watch Blondie do magic.

He looked magnificent, like a Titan rising from a volcano with flames licking his arms and his shoulders.

Knees bent, I circled the shifter as well, making sure to keep my distance. It worked in my favor that they wanted me alive, so I had a little wiggle room to fight and not worry he would bite my head off. Some of them were not aware of how strong they were and were known to cause irreparable damage accidently, according to the lectures Alex the Alpha had given me. The wolf lowered his head, pinning his ears close to his head and forcing my heart to skip a beat. I stumbled when the ground shook and groaned under our feet.

Flashes of lightning blinked from my left where Sissily was literally frying the shifter on a low simmer. Electric magic crackled in long ropes, zapping him left and right and making him yelp. She was doing good too, until at the last moment, the shifter jerked his body left but jumped at her from the right. The electric magic flew wide in the empty space, and my friend shrieked in surprise when the wolf tackled her. I was so focused on her, my heart in my throat,

I didn't see my opponent coming. Rookie mistake, but this was Sissily we were talking about. I couldn't just let her get hurt.

His heavy weight rammed me in the side, taking me down. My shoulder popped, bearing the brunt of the impact, and stars danced at the edges of my vision. Hot breath puffed on one side of my face, while my other cheek was being mushed in the damp soil. Counting on the jerk pinning me not to kill me since he needed me alive, I took a deep breath and flicked my fingers at the wolf snapping his jaws in Sissily's face.

Nothing happened.

"What the fuck." Gasping for air while my ribs were being crushed, I did it again.

Nothing.

How was it possible that I almost took Sissily's foot off by accident in the car, but I couldn't help her when her life was in danger? Had Hecate heard my plea and taken the magic away? Seriously? She couldn't wait until we were not about to die? What in the actual fuck?

Anger bubbled under my skin, heating it.

Lighting up like a box of firecrackers accidently set on fire, my sigils bloomed underneath my skin. The ground where I was pressed shook hard enough to push the wolf off me, yet my rage grew. I'd be damned if I gave it back after all the shit I'd been through from the day I was born. Dry earth crackled, chasms opening and spreading like cobwebs from where I was plastered on the dirt. A golden glow burst from my fingertips, reaching for the wolf who had his sharp teeth embedded in Sissily's forearm while she struggled to keep them away from her neck and face. Internally, I was cursing everything Hecate held dear, including all her precious witches. If my best friend died from being poisoned by a shifter's bite, I would make it my mission to fuck up everything that revered her name.

Halfway to the wolf, the golden glow of my insane magic billowed into a cloud instead of a wrist-sized rope, and the bright light dimmed. It paused in its movement like it was gathering strength, and I sucked in a breath when the yellow tones darkened from orange into bright red with veins of black through it. With one strong pulse like a heartbeat, it split in three and zapped each of the shifters. The main cloud rose higher, looming over my best friend and the feral wolf suspending itself there. A strange feeling that it was assessing the situation washed over me, but that couldn't be right. Magic didn't have a mind of its own; it only carried our intention with it.

Didn't it?

Fully focused on the menacing cloud drifting in the air, I didn't feel my lips move at first. When I did pay attention, I couldn't stop it if my life depended on it. Language spilled from my mouth that I'd never heard before and I shouldn't even be able to pronounce properly. Yet my tongue had no bones twisting and moving over the lilting foreign words like I'd spoken it my entire life. One second everything stood still.

Then the deep red magic dropped on the wolf, enveloping it completely without getting anywhere near my friend. Tortured howls ripped through the silent air, sending tremors through me. It felt like they lasted for an eternity, the shrieks from animals replaced by the screams of men. All that I watched unblinking, my lips moving and musical words spilling from them like a lullaby. When the tormented sounds stopped, so did the mutters coming from me. My body rolled twice when the magic returned like a bullet inside me, and the next thing I knew, River was lifting me off the ground.

"Hazel." His strong fingers bit into my shoulders as he shook me. "Hazel, can you hear me?"

"Ya." My groan was more a whimper than anything else.

"Can you stand?" There was something in his tone that snapped my eyes open.

River was kneeling next to me, holding my upper body up with a firm grip on my shoulders. Sissily stood behind him cradling her bleeding forearm to her chest, her blue peepers wary. My gaze dropped to River's brown eyes, which had the same emotion swirling in them. It was a hot poker in my chest. Knowing those I tried to protect feared me.

"I don't know what happened." Sounding weak and pathetic would've pissed me off any other time. "The shifters?"

But they didn't need to tell me. My eyes shifted from Blondie's face to over his shoulder where the wolf who attacked me stood. A neat pile of bones rose from the ground like a large anthill, their color dull like they belonged to something that'd been dead for a century. Twisting in River's hold, I found two more piles of the same, and no sign of our attackers.

"I will never hurt you." My comment was aimed at Sissily. "You know that right?"

"What kind of a dumb question is that? Of course I do." She didn't, though.

My best friend would've been in my face if she didn't fear me instead of using River as a barrier between us. Not that I could blame her. I would do the same in her shoes, but it sure smarted like a bitch knowing it. With a fist squeezing my throat, I wiggled out of River's hold and stood. His hand on my elbow helped when I swayed, but the moment I felt okay, I stepped away from him, too.

"I don't know why that happened." Arms wrapped around my middle, I kept glancing between the bone piles. "It wasn't working, you know." Darting desperate eyes at both of them in turn, I shivered, although I wasn't cold. Actually, I was burning up. "When I saw the shifter taking Sissily down, the magic was not working. I had nothing." It took a couple of swallows to wet my mouth and loosen my throat. "Then I got angry thinking she'd die and all I could do was watch. Then … the cloud …" I trailed off, turning away from them.

Neither of them said anything.

We were all lost in our thoughts when the corn stalks swayed a few feet away. "What in the name of all gods happened here?" Danika appeared through the greenery.

"We discovered an archeological site." My anger was misplaced, but I snapped at her anyway. "Do you like it?"

"She sure sounds like herself." Alex Greywood popped up from behind her his murmured mocking, and his eyes danced on his face in humor.

"Oh, goody. Since your dogs couldn't take me in, you came to do the job personally, huh?" My sneer took the alpha back, and the smile slipped from his face. "You should try it, see if you make a better, more artistic pile." My hand flopped wildly around, pointing at the bones while I struggled not to cry. My eyes burned with unshed tears.

"Are those your wolves?" River stepped up when a storm clouded the alpha's features. The mismatched eyes lit from inside his skull when he moved the piercing gaze from me to inspect what was left of the wolves.

"No," Alex growled low after he sniffed the air in a very

animalistic way. "I have not scented any of them in my territory until now."

"They were black." For some reason, it felt important to tell him that. "I knew they were not yours."

"You do pay attention, huh?" Some of the anger abated from him, but not all. "If they were black wolves, then we have a very big problem," he told Danika.

"Can we talk somewhere else? Where I can place wards?" River stepped between me and Alex for some unknown reason. Didn't he see that I was the monster? "We need to get out of the open."

"I saw the price they placed on her." My grandmother was pissed. "They wasted no time."

"Let's take this on to pack lands." Alex was already leaving, not waiting to see if we followed. "I'm parked on the other side of this field. Your car will be brought there, Hazel."

In a row like ducks, we trotted after the alpha in silence.

Chapter Seventeen

Pack lands were breathtaking, even in the middle of a crisis. Hundreds of acres of land surrounded by thick woods not too close to Cleveland were patrolled by shifters on two and four legs. Alex didn't take the safety of his people lightly, and I was grateful for it. No matter how many times I'd seen it, I still wondered how his son managed to get to my door that one time he got lost.

"I envy you, all this nature," River told Alex as the SUV rolled through the long stretch of road toward the alpha's home.

"We need to be free, and it placates the beast." Alex couldn't hide the pride in his tone, not that I blamed him.

I had my face pressed against the glass, my breath clouding it while I watched the homes and people we passed. All of them stopped whatever they were doing to raise their hand and acknowledge their alpha. In return, he waved too, returning their respectful greeting. I always held Alex Greywood in high regard, and I still would if I wasn't worried he would cash in the second he got a chance. My already truck load of trust issues just redoubled with the whole dumb magic revelation. Sissily sitting mutely next to me lost in her thoughts was like a knife being twisted in an already open wound.

There was so much I wanted to say to my best friend, yet the words stuck on my tongue, refusing to be voiced. Since that cursed book went nuts on me, many thoughts crossed my mind, along with emotions. The initial fear dissipated faster than expected, and it was replaced by relief. After spending my whole life wishing I belonged, all my dreams became a reality before I had time to blink.

I had magic.

I was no longer a dud. No longer an embarrassment.

When all that happiness and glee hit me, I never considered how others would react to the change. I'd be lying if I said I didn't want to see pride on Danika's face. Coming from a long line of very powerful witches, I saw her struggle with my existence. Her confession told a different story, making it like she had to put up a front for everyone and act up her disappointment, but I knew better. Every time magic was needed and I couldn't deliver, it was an insistent thorn in her side.

Everything was up in the air. I had no idea what to expect or how I'd be able to control something that refused to be leashed. A new type of fear creeped up in my soul after the display of intelligence my magic gave us in the middle of the field. In truth, I didn't want to share that tid-bit with Danika, but I had a feeling Sissily or River might. Still, I stayed silent and stared out the window.

Amber rushed down the few steps from the wraparound porch to greet us with a warm smile on her face. Like her name suggested, wild clouds of corkscrews in flame red danced around her shoulders. Alex was out and wrapping her in his arms before any of us exited the SUV.

"Welcome, welcome." The alpha's mate spread her arms wide like she wanted to hug us all at once. "Come on in. I just pulled out pies from the oven."

Their home was three stories and large enough to house an army. When shifters started popping out like jack in the boxes out of all the rooms, it became apparent why. Sissily and I visited the pack a few times on Alex's insistence, but this was our first time entering their home. And that was what it was. A home. Not simply a house.

"Amber, I would like you to stay," my grandmother told the sweet woman that fed us pies until we could barely breathe a few hours later.

After a nod from Alex, his mate joined us in his office, perching on the armrest of his chair. The rest of us were sprinkled on overstuffed chairs, and Danika was sitting primly alone on a loveseat. The mismatched furniture somehow matched Alex with his dual-toned eyes. It was him through and through. That was all the observing I could do before the air shifted, becoming more serious, more oppressive somehow.

"Alex is free to fill you in on everything I told him when I asked for his help," my grandmother started, and I shrunk further in the chair. "In that time, we had a new development, and I will need another favor, I'm afraid."

"If it's in my power, and I'm assuming this is about Hazel, everything in my disposal is yours. Just name it." There was not a second of hesitation in his voice.

I wanted to die.

"I knew something like this was a great possibility." Danika avoided my gaze, and an abyss opened in my chest.

"That her magic would somehow be unsealed. So, before I ask for help, I have a confession to make."

"Another one?" If I sounded accusing and angry, that was because I was. What now? Another soul contract? Was it mine this time?

She ignored me like I hadn't spoken.

"The day Hazel found your pup, I might've had something to do with it." My grandmother's chin jutted out, and she stared down the alpha with all the grace of a fucking queen. While telling him she might've stolen his child.

Alex Greywood stilled along with his mate, until Amber flicked her gaze between Danika's arrogant stance and me trying to blend in with the fabric of the chair while gaping at her in shock. The alpha's mate squeezed his forearm, and it was like flipping a switch. He relaxed and nodded at my grandmother to continue.

"Your child was never in danger, I swear it, on my life. I just needed you to see who Hazel is. That she would do anything, including harm herself, to help others. So, if a time like this came to pass, you wouldn't think twice about protecting her."

"After admitting to using my only son to play your games Witch, that is a tall order to ask." No expression crossed the Alpha's face. He was closed off as tight as a nun in an adult store.

"You would do anything for the blood of your blood. So would I."

Some unspoken conversation passed between them none of us were privy to. Their stare down ended when Amber spoke directly to me.

"Hazel, I would like you to stay here in our home until they fix this mess." Her dainty hand flicked between Alex and Danika. "Don't you look at me like that, Alex Greywood. If that was our boy, I would lie, cheat, and kill without remorse to make sure he was safe. I would do it for all our children, just as you would." She rounded on her mate when he lifted an eyebrow at her. "Hazel is a sweet girl." I almost swallowed my tongue. Sweet? What the actual fuck? "A little spitfire, but so am I. Isn't that what you told me just a day ago? That she reminds you of me when I was her age? We will give her a safe place to stay."

"Very well." Alex smiled indulgently at his mate, and she grinned back.

"Hang on a minute. I can't stay here." I jumped on my feet, my arms wide like I was trying to ward them off from attacking each other. "No. Just no, mm-kay? I'm a hazard to everyone, including myself. You guys should lock me in a basement if anything. In a cage." The way the alpha's brow creeped up his forehead was fascinating. "Cage." As if he didn't know what that was, I made a box with my hands in the air.

"We can speak freely among each other—"

"Hello," I cut Danika off, pointing an accusing finger at River. "All this shit started when he showed up like a bad omen in our coven. Ever crossed your mind that he is a snitch?"

Seeing Danika rub a hand down her face was like finding a unicorn. "I asked Mr. Blackman to join the coven personally. He agreed to join me so we could protect you better, Hazel."

"I had no coven until I answered your grandmother's request." River had a quirk at the corners of his full lips that rubbed me wrong. Like he knew something I didn't, and I was too dumb to figure it out. "I assure you, I report to no one but myself, and her."

"Are yours ever going to join this clusterfuck they left us

to deal with?" Alex addressed River, but Blondie just shrugged without comment. That earned him a shake of a head from the alpha.

I had no idea what they were talking about, and I was too busy convincing them they should put me down like a rabid animal. "Be that as it may, I am still too dangerous to be around anyone. This ... this thing"—My arms flopped around, thankfully without demolishing the house— "Is unpredictable. I'm not willing to place others at risk just to save my own ass."

"The Blackwood pack is in cahoots with the vampires." Alex leaned heavily on his desk, lacing his fingers. "The last seven to eight months, the rest of us have been putting out fires because of the vampire elders. If you think having three shifters from that pack after you is a coincidence, you are very mistaken, young lady."

"It's not just the vampires. The council members from the other covens demand her magic be tested, and if she's too dangerous they will want to destroy her." Danika just sharpened an executioner's ax like we were discussing the weather. "The grapevine is whispering about the Fae coming from their hidey hole, as well."

My ass hit the chair when my legs gave out.

"You started it by pulling aces from your sleeve." Alex accused her, but he was staring at River.

Danika nodded in confirmation.

"I'm missing something here." Sissily was mute and of no help to me at all. "What are we talking about?"

"That is a discussion for another day. We have a lot to do if we are to prepare ourselves." My grandmother stood with the grace of a gazelle. "Double your guards, and tighten up ship so no one without your explicit green light enters your land. I'm sure I don't need to stress how important it is to stay on our guard right now." Alex nodded and stood too. "River and Sissily will be coming with me for now because I can use all the help I can get at the moment."

"We will guard her with our lives, Danika. You will be in debt to me and my pack for this." They clasped hands while I watched, too stunned to argue or say anything.

"The moment we have news, you'll hear from me and let's make it the other way around, please."

Curled on the chair lost and confused, I watched Amber hug everyone, including River, before they left the alpha's office. Sissily paused at the door, her gaze locked on me as her mouth opened and closed a few times, and then a tear trickled down her cheek before she rushed out of the room. There was no stopping the fat droplets rolling down my cheeks either, so I sniffled pathetically, until only Amber and I were left in the room.

She kneeled next to the chair I used as a bastion for my misery. "You will be fine, dear. I'm sure everything is too much now, but it takes time to adjust to any change. If you need to talk, you know my ear is always ready."

"I can't live with myself if I hurt anyone." Admitting my greatest fear was easy to the sweet woman. Her kind face held no pity, just understanding, which helped. "I-I can't control it. It has a mind of its own and reacts to my emotions."

"Which makes the pack a perfect place to be." At my confused bewilderment to her words, she laughed. "Have you seen hormonal teenagers before their initiation in the pack as adult shifters?" My lips twitched despite the dread trying to drown me. "We are the best teachers you will find when it comes to controlling your emotions and instincts. I'll tell you what. Starting tomorrow, I will train with you on how to control them, but you will have to cook with me at least twice a week. Deal?"

"Maybe I won't have to stay here that long." It was pathetic to hear the hopeful tone riding my words.

"However long it may be."

"Deal." Tears still rolled down my cheeks, but I smiled when she hugged me. Apart from Sissily, no one else had hugged me like that.

"It figures I'd be missing out on the good part of this meeting." Alex strode back in his office with a padded envelope tucked under his arm. "Do I get a hug too?" Smirking at his face, he pretended to be hurt when she swatted him.

"If you don't need her, I'd like to have a walk-through of the room with Hazel so she can pick a room." Amber looked at me with the hope of a two-year-old expecting a new toy.

"Go do your female things as long as I don't have to sit for hours while my nails are painted." Alex shivered, and I couldn't help myself. I barked out a laugh.

"Our daughters did that to him when they were young." Amber giggled, gazing adoringly at the burly guy.

"Before I forget, this came for you." The alpha shoved the envelope at me.

"For me?" Eyeing it like it'd bite me, I took a step back. "No one knows I'm here. I didn't know I'd be here."

Alex frowned at the package in his hands before stomping to his desk. Amber moved closer, tucking her arm at my elbow, and we watched him rip it open. When he shook it, a familiar thing fell on his desk with a solid thump. We all stared at it in silence, until Alex picked it up and turned it over in his fingers.

"Is this yours?" The book that caused all of the shit in my life looked so small in his large hand.

I swallowed the lump choking me. "Yes." My croak rasped through my lips.

"Why are you looking at it like you've seen a ghost?" No wonder Alex was puzzled. He had no idea.

"Because it burned with the rest of the books in the library at dawn," I admitted.

"Maybe it's a sign, Hazel," Amber muttered under her breath. "From what I understood, this book set your magic free." She giggled at my surprise. "I watch videos on my phone too while waiting on something to finish baking. I read the comments about what happened to you. Maybe the book is not done with you yet."

That's what I was afraid of. How much more damage could it do? Tilting my head, I reached for it, plucking it out of Alex's fingers. It didn't blast me with light, nor did it try to rearrange my organs.

"Amber, you said you'd teach me control, right?"

"I did, yes." The woman had a ready smile for anyone.

"Maybe we should start today." I had no time to dwell in misery and self-pity. If they wanted my head on a spike, I'd be ready to bite their hands off before they touched me. All the time I'd wished for magic, I didn't think it'd have me running for my life. Nonetheless, I had it now, and I would do anything to have it do my bidding.

As for the demons?

I guess Leviathan was very determined to get his claws on my grandmother's soul.

He better be ready for a fight too, because he wouldn't know what hit him when I got my hands on his demonic ass.

It was time for me to take my place in the world of magic.

Hecate help whoever stood in my way.

Next in the Chronicles of Forbidden Witchery Series

vinci-books.com/pitchawitch

Some witches master spells—I specialize in catastrophes.

A demon ate my Prada shirt, my spastic magic makes me supernatural bait, and now I'm shackled to River Blackman—an arrogant bastard with deadly secrets. If his skeletons break loose, we're both doomed.

Turn the page for a free preview…

Pitch A Witch: Chapter One

"No." That one word stung like a slap across my face.

Bristling at the blatant refusal, my arms folded across my chest like they had a mind of their own. Standing in Alex Greywood's home office was not my favorite pastime on the worst of days, but it was a solid plan to get my ass out of pack lands and back where I belonged. Unfortunately, I had to act like a ten-year-old having a tantrum, but a girl had to do what a girl had to do.

"They"—Speaking slowly and deliberately, I narrowed my eyes at the alpha, who was scowling down his nose at me — "owe me a Mercedes SLK55. It's a convertible, might I remind you. I have every right to demand they compensate me for my way-over-one-hundred-thousand-dollar car ... in person." My forefinger snapped at his face like a whip on that last part.

With a tortured groan that made me think the conversation was causing him physical pain, Alex shook his head at me. "I know how much that car costs. Hazel, but we need to deal with the vampires delicately, as you well know. We can't demand anything if we are trying to convince them not to amalgamate with the demons and to leave you alone. It's your life we are talking about here, woman. You must work with me on this."

"Tell that to my poor car. They pulverized it, Alex." Widening my peepers to get my point across better, I slammed my fist on his desk for emphasis. We both knew this had nothing to do with the vehicle or how much it cost since that was small potatoes for Danika's bank account, but the great person he was, the alpha played along with it ... for the moment.

"Pulverized it." His mouth twisted as if me repeating that fact was a foul stench drifting up his nose while I grinded my fist into the palm of my other hand to add a visual experience. "As in smashed it like it owed them a life debt. Its guts were sprinkled all over the road, too. You can check it out for yourself if you don't believe me, since it's used as a scarecrow in the middle of a freaking cornfield now."

A soft click announced the door of the office opening, and Amber poked her head inside, brightening the moment her eyes landed on her mate. He dropped the glower as well, turning his body toward her like she was the sun in his solar system and he gravitated toward it subconsciously. It was always as disgusting as it was fascinating to see how much these two loved each other. And I meant disgusting in the sweetest possible way. Anyone around them wished to find a connection like that, but rarely anyone got lucky enough to experience it.

One thing I knew for sure was I'd never find that in my lifetime.

"I can come back later if you two are busy," Amber addressed Alex, but her warm smile was aimed at me.

I curled the corners of my lips tightly in return, fighting the need to squirm. I adored the redhead more than anyone else and didn't deserve her kindness. With her presence, my plan to get back to my house had gone down the drain, however. Guilt drilled a hole in my stomach from the thought.

"No, no. Please come in, my love. Maybe you can talk some sense into her," Alex huffed, waving a hand toward me as if there was another idiot standing inside his office with us and he needed to point out who he was talking about. "She's as stubborn as any other female in this house. It's like talking to a brick wall. Are we absolutely certain she's not a shifter?"

"Why is it that I'm being called stubborn for refusing to let them get away with constantly causing unnecessary damage to others?" Turning from Alex to Amber, I raised my eyebrows all the way to my hairline. "Do you know what I've had to sacrifice because of demons and vampires lately? Do you?"

"Is this about the boots, again? I swear to the full moon I will start howling if I hear one more thing about shoes or clothing," the alpha snarled at me, his finger pointed accusingly at my face.

Amber snickered, stepping inside and closing the door. I watched her from the corner of my eye as she moved to join him behind the long wooden desk while I continued my argument, disregarding the little tid-bit that I was an adult woman and not a snotty child.

"They were designer boots, as I've pointed out many times. You are a guy, so of course you don't sympathize with my pain on that matter." My pout made a muscle twitch under his green eye. The blue one shot daggers at me. "I just bought them, too." Was I acting like a sullen toddler? Why, yes. Yes, I was.

"Sit down, love." Amber patted her mate on the chest and, none too gently, shoved him in the leather chair. He huffed and narrowed his gaze on her but wisely stayed silent. "We don't want you to burst a blood vessel while Hazel here is trying to find a way to leave pack lands."

"What ... I ... I would never." Stuttering and acting appalled at the accusations, I made the mistake of laying it on too thick. "I'm not dumb to leave when I'm safe and protected here."

I winced.

I should've just stopped at "never."

Damn it.

"Like you didn't try to sneak out yesterday when the patrol found you trying to hot-wire one of the vehicles?" Amber giggled good-naturedly, but a storm darkened her mate's face as his eyes drilled holes in my face from across the desk.

My mouth opened and closed, yet nothing came out of it. Admitting defeat was never easy for me, but I had it on good authority that this battle wouldn't be won if what I knew about Alex Greywood was true. Not at that moment anyway. So, shrewdly I shrugged and toed the edge of the rug with my shoe like a teenager. It was painful to see my master plan backfire.

"If I say I was testing how effective your beta's teams were when on patrol, would you believe me?" With a syrupy smile plastered on my face, I mockingly fluttered my eyelashes at the alpha. I was going out of my freaking mind. He knew it, I knew it, and the entire fucking pack knew I was ready to peel off my own skin from frustration.

Instead of shouting, reprimanding, or even kicking me

out as any other person with a brain would've done in his place after my obnoxious behavior, Alex slouched in the chair with a sigh. "Why?" was all he asked, and it came out in a low, even tone while he rubbed a hand over his face.

"It's been eight days, nine hours, and thirty-four minutes, Alex. No one has returned with any answers or a fucking solution to my little problem here." His arched eyebrow chafed at me badly.

Not even Amber shaking her head at me in disappointment could change the fact that I was miserable enough to risk death just so I could join Sissily out there. I missed my friend more than anything else, although she probably hated my guts after seeing what kind of a freak I was.

"Yes, I've been counting, damn it. You would be, too, if you had to hide like a coward while everyone you care about is risking their life out there."

"Who are you and what did you do to Hazel?" Astonished, I gaped as he peered at me with a small smile playing at the corners of his mouth.

It took my brain a moment to register that he'd joked to lessen the tension radiating from me. Ever since I was deposited on his doorstep like some unwanted offspring, I worked hard daily to learn about the unexpected magic I suddenly had. Be it with Amber in the mornings where she did everything to make me comfortable with all the emotional changes happening inside my body, or with a multitude of shifters, including their alpha, to keep me in top physical shape so I didn't succumb to my powers. I still felt trapped, no matter what little progress I'd made or whatever fun I had, by the fact I was no longer a dud.

I gave him a flat, unimpressed look.

"I understand how you feel, I really do," Alex expressed with a measured tone, and Amber hummed in agreement from where she was perched comfortably on his lap. Good thing she sat on him because I had no doubt he would jump over the desk and strangle me otherwise. "It's never easy to sit back while others take control of the wheel, but this is only temporary. The deeper we dig into what is going on with the demons, the more invested I am as well. All this frustration because you think you're not doing anything is just the calm before the storm. I've seen it more times than I can count."

"I'm losing my mind, Alex." My nails scraped my scalp harshly as I started pacing. "Danika is in her own world playing a dictator and making sure everyone dances to her tune, but the truth of the matter is, all of you are in danger because of me. Call me an idiot, but I'm not going to sit and be obedient just to make her or anyone else happy. I should be out there figuring this out with everyone else."

Mismatched eyes rolled over me with a calculating glint that did not bode well for me. After Danika dropped a shit ton of bombs in this very office, she took Blondie and my best friend, and I had yet to hear a word from any of them. River staying away from me was a great thing. I didn't trust the pretty boy now any more than I did the first time I'd laid eyes on him. All my girly parts were having a blast from him being around, though my trust issues slapped that nonsense away fast enough, thank Hecate. But Sissily? I needed to talk to her. To apologize for what I was, or for my incompetence to control the magic I never knew I had. To tell her something.

Anything really.

I felt lost, and more than anything, I was afraid I'd lost the only person who always had my back no matter how bad things turned out. Each night since she walked out the door and left me behind without saying a word, her fearful expression had haunted my nightmares. I'd live with everyone hating me, or even being made fun of by every witch in existence. I just wanted my friend back.

"I'll make you a deal." Alex waited while I struggled to inflate my lungs. "If no one comes to give us news by Friday, I'm taking you with me to pay your coven a visit."

It was Monday morning.

"By Wednesday." Holding his gaze, I countered, doing everything in my power not to gnaw on my lip when the full power of an alpha stare stabbed my pupils.

With a chuckle, he planted a kiss on Amber's shoulder, then grinned at me. "You fit perfectly in this house. Thursday, and not a day sooner."

"I feel wonderful that I need to resort to childish behavior so I can do what's right, just so you know." Grimacing, I turned toward the door, eager to leave before I died from embarrassment.

"Not that fast, dear." Amber's voice made me pause with one hand on the doorknob, the door opened just a crack. "As you said, it's been eight days, and you are yet to cook with me."

"I knew something was going to bite me in the ass from this conversation, I just didn't know what." Beaming at her when she giggled, I waited by the open door for her to join me.

"We have a pack gathering this evening, so we better get started."

Alex guffawed at my horrified expression. His barking laughter followed us to the kitchen like a theme song announcing our entrance inside a fight ring.

Grab your copy...
vinci-books.com/pitchawitch

About the Author

Maya Daniels, USA Today Bestselling and multi-award-winning supernatural suspense author, is a fun-loving woman with many talents.

She traveled the world, gaining life experiences that helped her career as an investigative journalist, as well as her storytelling. Maya writes compelling tales of magic, mythical creatures, loyalty, and life-changing friendships with snarky female characters—much like herself.

Her travels have taken her to Europe, Africa, Asia, Australia, and America. Born with her feet in motion, she currently resides in Ohio, spinning her next epic story that you will not want to put down.

Her biggest 'sins' are her love of chocolate and coffee—through an IV drip! One to never sit still, Maya practices Reiki healing, different types of martial arts, reads about the arcane, talks to furry creatures more than humans, picks up a sledgehammer for home improvement, and travels with her fated mate, seeking her own adventures.

www.ingramcontent.com/pod-product-compliance
Ingram Content Group UK Ltd.
Pitfield, Milton Keynes, MK11 3LW, UK
UKHW040035130426
469799UK00003B/118